P9-CPY-576

When The Stick Turned Blue, October's *Man Of The Month* Turned White!

Flint had just conceded that coming to New York after Ashlinn had been a mistake when the bright blue-and-white box in her bathroom's trash can caught his eye. The words printed on the box seemed to leap into Flint's line of vision: *Pregnancy Test.* To burn into his consciousness. Nothing could have prevented him from picking up that box. From reading every word on it.

He heard a small gasp and looked up to see Ashlinn standing a few feet away, wearing old ripped jeans and a faded Yankees baseball shirt.

Flint spotted the plastic stick with the test result and snatched it up. "Congratulations. According to this, you're going to be a mother. When were you going to tell me?"

Dear Reader,

Welcome to Silhouette Desire—where you're guaranteed powerful, passionate and provocative love stories that feature rugged heroes and spirited heroines who experience the full emotional intensity of falling in love!

This October you'll love our new MAN OF THE MONTH title by Barbara Boswell, *Forever Flint*. Opposites attract when a city girl becomes the pregnant bride of a millionaire outdoorsman.

Be sure to "rope in" the next installment of the exciting Desire miniseries TEXAS CATTLEMAN'S CLUB with *Billionaire Bridegroom* by Peggy Moreland. When cattle baron Forrest Cunningham wants to wed childhood friend Becky Sullivan, she puts his love to an unexpected test.

The always-wonderful Jennifer Greene returns to Desire with her magical series HAPPILY EVER AFTER. *Kiss Your Prince Charming* is a modern fairy tale starring an unforgettable "frog prince." In a sexy battle-of-the-sexes tale, Lass Small offers you *The Catch of Texas*. Anne Eames continues her popular miniseries MONTANA MALONES with *The Unknown Malone*. And Sheri WhiteFeather makes her explosive Desire debut with *Warrior's Baby*, a story of surrogate motherhood with a twist.

Next month, you'll really feel the power of the passion when you see our new provocative cover design. Underneath our new covers, you will still find six exhilarating journeys into the seductive world of romance, with a guaranteed happy ending!

Enjoy!

Joan Marlow Golan
Senior Editor, Silhouette Desire

Please address questions and book requests to:
Silhouette Reader Service
U.S.: 3010 Walden Ave., P.O. Box 1325, Buffalo, NY 14269
Canadian: P.O. Box 609, Fort Erie, Ont. L2A 5X3

BARBARA BOSWELL

loves writing about families. "I guess family has been a big influence on my writing," she says. "I particularly enjoy writing about how my characters' family relationships affect them."

When Barbara isn't writing and reading, she's spending time with her *own* family—her husband, three daughters and three cats, whom she concedes are the true bosses of their home! She has lived in Europe, but now makes her home in Pennsylvania. She collects miniatures and holiday ornaments, tries to avoid exercise and has somehow found the time to write over twenty category romances.

One

"I was told to look for the Paradise Outdoors sign at the gate. I'm Ash…"

"*You're* Asher Carey?" Flint Paradise stared at the dark-haired, dark-eyed young woman standing before him and the sign he held, Paradise Outdoors, spelled out in bold black letters.

"That can't be right," he replied to his own question.

Asher was definitely a male name, wasn't it? Of course, these days, who knew? But she had to be in her twenties, and in the decade she'd been born in, parents had sensibly reserved masculine names for boys. Hadn't they?

"No, my name is Ashlinn and…"

"I figured you weren't Asher Carey." Flint was relieved. It was imperative that she not be. He was here at the Sioux Falls airport to meet the flight of Asher Carey, the writer for *Tour & Travel* magazine, the *male* writer booked for the two-week Paradise Outdoors Company expedition.

"I'm from *Tour & Travel* magazine in New York, here for the Paradise Outdoors expedition," she interjected.

This couldn't be! Flint urgently flipped through the papers affixed to his clipboard. The name *Asher Carey* headed one sheet.

"See, here it is. Asher." Flint showed her the paper, pointing at the name. "*He's* the one booked on the trip."

"Yes, it does say Asher," Ashlinn Carey conceded with a shrug. "Maybe it's a typo or something. I can show you all kinds of ID proving that I'm Ashlinn Carey and that I am with *Tour & Travel.* If you'd care to call the publisher, he will assure you this assignment is all mine."

She appeared unflappable. No wonder. She considered the mixup to be a minor error. A *typo!* It was so much more than that, Flint decided grimly. What they were facing was a catastrophic case of mistaken identity. For not only was Ashlinn Carey a woman, she was a very pretty woman—and by the looks of her, a hip urban type who would be about as comfortable in the wild as a buffalo would be in a New York City magazine office.

And he was supposed to take *her* and four men besides himself camping in the Black Hills of Custer State Park for two weeks? Two weeks in the outdoors with an out-of-her-element city girl? Who looked…delicious, even after a long flight complete with layovers in two airports? Flint half expected his life to flash before his eyes, like a drowning victim going down for the last time.

The two stood facing each other.

"I don't know how something like this could have happened," Flint growled as he permitted himself another covert perusal of her, noting every one of her attributes.

There were many. Thick shiny hair, almost jet-black in color, sleek and straight and shoulder length. Wide-set coffee-brown eyes framed by dark lashes and brows. Good features, good face. He guessed that she'd never gone through an awkward, unattractive stage in her life. His kid sister Eva had been like that—adorable baby, darling kid, cute teen and, ultimately, pretty woman. But no further references to Eva applied, because the fierce jolt of arousal that suddenly struck him as he stared at Ashlinn Carey had nothing to do with brotherly admiration and everything to do with…well, arousal. Attraction. If he believed in the schoolboy fantasy of lust at first sight— which he didn't, of course—it probably would feel a lot like this.

Flint tried to divert his unexpected attack of desire by redirecting his thoughts to something else. Something suitably distracting. He conjured up quick mental images of his teenaged half sisters, Camryn and Kaylin, who could always be counted on to infuriate him. But the mental trick didn't work; the girls' powers of annoyance faded in comparison to Ashlinn Carey's considerable sensual draw.

He continued to gaze at her. The burgundy lipstick she wore looked freshly applied, perhaps moments before the plane had landed. The color accentuated the full, fine shape of her lips. She was wearing a one-piece black jersey outfit and a pair of ultra-fashionable black boots that added a few inches to her height. Still, at nearly six-four, he was considerably taller than she.

"You're supposed to be a guy," he said hoarsely.

How he wished she were! Barring that, it would've helped a lot if she didn't have such an eye-popping figure, if she were one of those unappealing living toothpicks currently showcased in ads. Instead, Ashlinn Carey was soft and curvy in all the right places and projected a sultry allure without even trying. His skin felt uncomfortably warm, his entire body taut.

Ashlinn surveyed him coolly. "Well, I'm not a guy, am I? Are you Sam Carmody?"

"No."

"You're supposed to be."

Flint assumed she was needling him with her argument about his identity, since he'd just done the same thing to her. "I guess I had that coming," he grumbled.

"My trip packet clearly states that Sam Carmody, the director of marketing for Paradise Outdoors, who is also in charge of this expedition, will meet my plane at the airport," Ashlinn insisted.

"Carmody is in the hospital in traction for the next three weeks. Skateboard accident. The idiot," Flint muttered under his breath before he could catch himself.

"You're not very sympathetic. Three weeks in traction sounds awful."

"I've been trying to be sympathetic since I got the bad news last night. But all I can think of is that any thirty-two-year-old man who tries to skateboard down the front steps of the high school is an idiot." Flint grimaced. "I'm only a year older than he is, and I wouldn't dream of going near a skateboard. Especially one day before the camping trip that's been his own pet project from the start."

"To be perfectly honest, I think I'd rather be in traction myself than to go to a place called the Badlands. I mean, the name itself says it all, doesn't it? What can be good about going there?" Ashlinn smiled for the first time. "Since the trip is canceled, I'll just book a flight back to New York and…"

"The trip is still on. The other four guys have already arrived and are raring to go. I'm the new leader of the pack, so to speak."

Flint dragged his eyes away from her, a defensive move on his part because her smile had affected him tangibly, like a blow upside the head. He felt queerly disoriented.

Flint was appalled. And bewildered. First, the sight of her set his body on fire, then her smile literally dazed him. What was going on here? he wondered with a consternation mingled with alarm. He had never been the emotional type, succumbing to the impulses of a hot and instant physical attraction. He was a thinker, a planner, rational and controlled.

The last time he'd been goaded into acting on impulse…

Flint frowned, remembering last year's folly when his twin brother, Rafe, had persuaded him to pick up a blond business-woman in a downtown hotel coffee shop. Within an hour, he had been back in his office, without ever laying a hand—or anything else—on the woman. He'd recognized that it was

Rafe's ribbing, not his own attraction to the blonde that had prompted his actions, and swiftly ended the impetuous date.

But Rafe hadn't chided him about the lack of women in his life for months. In fact, Rafe was so absorbed in his new marriage that Flint doubted that he even noticed his twin's lack of a social life. No, he couldn't blame his inconvenient impulses toward Ashlinn Carey on his brother.

Flint's frown deepened. "Anyway, we're not going to the Badlands, we're going to the Black Hills. Since you've obviously not done your homework for this assignment, let me clue you in—they're two different places."

"Oh." Ashlinn's face flushed. "I… I was only recently given this assignment."

"Sure." Flint made it clear that he didn't believe her. Great, just great. In addition to everything else, she was a slacker. As a devout workaholic, he couldn't abide such behavior.

Ashlinn was looking none too pleased herself.

"Four other *guys* are taking this trip?" she asked succinctly. "I'm supposed to spend two weeks on an all-male adventure into the wild?"

Flint shrugged. "We took it for granted this trip was for men only. What woman reads a magazine like *Tour & Travel?* So why would they even have women writers on the staff?"

"Have you ever read *Tour & Travel?*" demanded Ashlinn. "Most of it is geared toward professional women who enjoy interesting weekend getaways and vacations to charming little places where…"

"Are you sure we're talking about the same magazine? Carmody showed me a copy, and it was geared toward—well, guys like Carmody."

"Thirty-two-year-old idiots who skateboard with teenagers," Ashlinn said darkly.

"Men who are free from domestic responsibilities and have a penchant for adventure and challenge," Flint found himself lapsing into the marketing-speak of Carmody himself. "And who also have plenty of disposable income to spend on the specialty items that Paradise Outdoors sells."

"And that would be skateboards and other toys for the alleged adult male?" Ashlinn inquired sarcastically.

"Let's stick to your magazine and its focus—whatever that is," countered Flint. "For starters, redefine what you mean by 'charming.' Because if it involves things like running water and gourmet dinners and shopping, none of those were in last month's issue of *Tour & Travel.*"

"Oh no, last month's issue!" Ashlinn heaved a groan. "I'd actually managed to forget about it. Or maybe it's simply pure denial. That issue was the first one to come out under the…new publisher. He's changed the entire format, the entire concept of the magazine. Everything is different now."

"I see. Sort of." Flint gazed quizzically at her. "That still doesn't explain why the magazine sent you out here. I can't imagine that Carmody wasn't clear about this being an all-male excursion."

"Well, I guess the 'Asher' could have been a typo. But I'm becoming more and more convinced that he—Presley Oakes Jr., the new publisher of *T & T*—did this on purpose." Ashlinn's deep-brown eyes flashed fire. "It would be exactly like him to pull a stunt like this, first assigning me to write an article, then making it about a testosterone-fueled trip into some godforsaken wilderness."

"I'm gonna go out on a limb here and say that you don't much care for your new boss," Flint said dryly.

She drew a sharp breath. "I was a senior editor at the magazine until Junior's father bought it and turned it over to him. Do you know what it's like to work for a boss who's just celebrated his twenty-third birthday?"

"Twenty-three, huh?" Flint wondered what response she was expecting. Weren't women notoriously touchy about their age? He cleared his throat. "Er, I guess that makes him younger than you?"

"Duh!"

"I was trying to be tactful," Flint defended himself.

"You needn't bother. I'm not ashamed of my age, which is five years older than Junior. Five pivotal, crucial years!"

"I'm guessing things got off to a rocky start when Junior took the helm," Flint surmised. "So he's making a senior editor write about a camping trip, and to top it off, he sends a female to go with a bunch of guys. Yeah, things are beginning to fall into place now." Flint nodded his head knowingly. "Too bad Paradise Outdoors got dragged into Junior's scheme to get rid of you. Wait until I talk to Carmody! He should've picked up on the…"

"There is no scheme to get rid of me!" cried Ashlinn.

"No?" Flint arched his brows. "If you're so secure in your position, then why didn't you refuse this assignment? It doesn't sound like you were very enthused about it, even before you got here and found out it was men only."

"That's not true, I…"

"Shall I quote yourself to you? 'The Badlands, the name itself says it all'…'what can be good about going there?' Let's not forget 'some godforsaken wilderness.' And then there was your unsurpassed glee when you assumed the trip was canceled. You actually smiled."

He remembered the flash of sexual heat her smile had inspired in him. He'd better make sure that didn't happen again.

Ashlinn's shoulders slumped. "Okay, you're right. I wasn't looking forward to the trip. And I…didn't do much reading about the state of South Dakota so I thought the Black Hills were *in* the Badlands, not separate areas. No offense."

"None taken. Not too much, anyway. So you felt you couldn't just say no when you were given the assignment?"

"One doesn't say 'no' to Junior and still have a job. So far I've survived the purge that followed his takeover." She heaved a sigh.

"Sounds bad. Why haven't you quit?" Flint was genuinely curious.

She made a wry face. "I have this practical side that asserts itself, reminding me that I can't afford to be unemployed. I've barely made a dent in my student loans and I have other key bills to pay—you know, like food and rent. I'd really hate to give up eating and live on the streets."

"Cheer up, this expedition should definitely broaden your options. You'll learn survival skills so you can live off the land."

"Is that supposed to be funny?"

"Well, yes." Flint's lips twitched. "I thought a little humor couldn't hurt."

"You might notice that I'm not laughing." She glowered at him.

There was nothing remotely humorous about her predicament, Ashlinn mused glumly. As if this assignment from the little weasel who'd pronounced *T & T*'s format—and staff—stale and stodgy and too *old* weren't bad enough, it was now quite clear that she was unwelcome on the expedition. The group leader was as eager to be rid of her as Junior was to replace her at *Tour & Travel* with one of his young buddies.

Well, she wasn't going to give either one the satisfaction of her quitting!

Ashlinn clutched her overnight bag so tightly that her fingers ached. To say that she hadn't been looking forward to this trip was definitely an understatement. She'd always loathed Carey family camping vacations while growing up, and as an adult gladly avoided places where sleeping bags, cooking over an open fire and applying mosquito repellent by the quart were required.

Now this. Plus, she was to be the only female among a gang of would-be Daniel Boones bent on exploring the wilderness with high-tech gadgets and equipment. Could it get any worse?

It could.

"We're scheduled to leave at dawn tomorrow," said Flint.

"Dawn?" Ashlinn echoed, dismayed. "Why so early? It's not like the Badlands—uh, the Black Hills—are going anywhere. They'll still be there if we leave at a decent hour in the morning."

"Dawn is the decent hour to begin this trip," Flint said firmly. "We have to drive nearly the length of the state to reach the campgrounds."

Ashlinn glanced at her watch. It was already past ten—and

that was Central Time. Her body was still operating on Eastern Standard Time, which made it a whole hour later.

"Where's the baggage claim?" she asked wearily. "I'll collect my luggage and then we can get out of here." She was booked into a motel tonight and wanted nothing more than to fall into bed and try to get some sleep before the odious dawn departure.

"Luggage?"

"You look as if you're unfamiliar with the concept." Ashlinn's patience was wearing very thin.

"How much luggage?" His testy tone matched hers.

"Just two suitcases," she began defensively. "I..."

"Well, you'll have to leave them behind. We're only bringing what we can carry in the extended-journey-size backpacks. Everybody is receiving identical ones, courtesy of Paradise Outdoors."

Ashlinn stared at the man who was not marketing chief Sam Carmody. His eyes, black as obsidian chips, were watching her closely, no doubt to gauge her reaction to his latest pronouncement. He was openly trying to discourage her; he was still hoping that she would bail out of the torturous fate awaiting her.

Not that she didn't want to.

But that practical side of her nature dismissed the misery of rising before dawn and lugging a heavy-duty backpack through rugged terrain. She really had no choice. The raise she'd been counting on had fallen through when *Tour & Travel* had been sold, and her living expenses seemed to be increasing, though she'd actually cut back her spending. She hadn't eaten out once since Presley Oakes Jr. took over the magazine, and in a city of great restaurants like New York, that was a cruel hardship indeed.

But the prospect of unemployment was far worse.

If she were fired, the benefits she would be eligible for wouldn't come close to making ends meet. And if she quit her job, she wouldn't get a cent from anywhere. Either way, she would have to leave New York...

She couldn't leave New York, she wouldn't! Ashlinn re-
solved once again. She loved the city; living there had always
been her dream and an obnoxious little twerp like Presley
Oakes Jr. wasn't going to drive her away. Neither was the
replacement for the hapless Sam Carmody.

She was going on this trip, she would write the wretched
article and keep her job. She would show this outdoor fanatic
that she could survive in the wilderness, and when she returned
to the office she would outlast Junior, who was bound to grow
bored playing a magazine publisher. As it was, he had nothing
in common with the adults on the *T & T* staff, and seemed to
spend most of his time at work playing computer games in his
office.

An invigorating wave of hostility washed over her. "Who
are you, anyway?" she demanded.

"Flint Paradise, president and CEO of Paradise Outdoors."

"And you have the time to take over the role of group leader
into the wild, even though you're the president and CEO of a
company?" She regarded him suspiciously. "Doesn't sound
like your presence is exactly vital to your business. Or maybe
your company doesn't do much business? Is this trip a desperation measure to garner some kind of…"

"Paradise Outdoors is having a banner year," Flint cut in
testily. She'd clearly struck a nerve with her jibes at his company. "Furthermore, I'm viewing the next two weeks as a paid
vacation, the first I've ever taken."

"Translation—you couldn't get anybody else to go,"
taunted Ashlinn. "That certainly bodes well for this trip."

Flint was irked. How had she guessed that his entire senior
staff had opted out of the trip, citing irrevocable family plans
and obligations, an excuse they knew *he* couldn't give? Still,
he was loathe to admit that to her.

"Why wouldn't I take advantage of an all-expenses-paid
trip? Because the entire expedition, including guide fees, has
been bankrolled by *your* magazine."

Ashlinn was momentarily taken aback. "It has?"

"It has." Flint started walking toward the baggage claim area.

Automatically, Ashlinn trotted alongside him. "Junior didn't mention that *Tour & Travel* was financing the trip."

"Well, you are. Carmody arranged the logistics of the expedition, but *Tour & Travel* is footing the bill for everybody. Paradise Outdoors will also get a year's free advertising in the magazine and publicity for the products used, because you'll be writing about them in your article."

They came to stand beside a revolving carousel, waiting for the luggage to appear.

"Let me make sure I have this right—*Tour & Travel* is funding this camping trip *and* giving the Paradise Outdoors Company free advertising for a year plus free publicity for products sold by the company?" Ashlinn said carefully. "What exactly does the magazine get out of this deal?"

"That's what I asked Carmody." Flint shrugged. "He told me the publisher said *Tour & Travel* wanted the article badly and thought it was worth paying for."

"I see." Boy did she ever! Junior hates me and is hoping I'll either quit or get permanently lost in the wilderness, Ashlinn thought grimly. He'd consider *that* worth paying for, especially since it was his daddy's money, not his own, that he was throwing around.

"Carmody had all the proper contracts signed so I had no objections to this trip—until now," Flint added, narrowing his eyes. "Now, I not only have objections, I have grave reservations."

"Oh, I had those from the start," muttered Ashlinn.

They watched in silence as baggage from the flight began to slide down the chute onto the carousel. Ashlinn quickly claimed hers, two matching top-brand suitcases that she'd purchased on sale. She was an excellent shopper, tracking down bargains, finding quality merchandise at the lowest prices. It was a talent that wouldn't come in too handy on this particular trip, she acknowledged ruefully.

"Let's go." Flint handed her his clipboard and his sign and lifted a suitcase in each hand. He grimaced at the weight.

She decided to beat him to the punch with, "Go on, make the predictable tired old quip about rocks being in there. How about asking me if I packed everything but the kitchen sink?"

"Did you?" He headed toward the doors. "Now it's your turn to laugh politely at the lame joke."

"Ha, ha," she said. "Was that polite enough?"

Though he carried the two heavy bags, he was striding along at a rate that made her half run to keep up with him. They left the terminal and headed toward the parking area, eventually reaching a champagne-colored Saturn.

Flint proceeded to load her bags into the trunk.

"I guess we won't be taking this car into the Bad Hills," Ashlinn said. She sounded nervous, even to herself.

She *was* nervous. Because it had just occurred to her that she was expected to climb inside this car with this man, whom she hardly knew. At night, in an unfamiliar city. She was too well-versed in stranger danger not to be uneasy. Alarm quickly followed. What should she do?

"That would be the Black Hills," corrected Flint. He opened the passenger door for her and stood there, waiting for her to get in. "And you guessed right. My car stays home. We're taking a big van with four-wheel drive and tires sturdy enough for the roughest terrain."

Ashlinn hesitated beside the door and began to leaf through the pages on the clipboard, stalling for time. She couldn't bring herself to move, let alone get into the car where the two of them would be alone together in the darkness.

She skipped over the 'Asher Carey' page and read aloud the names on the other four sheets. "Jack Hall. Etienne Bouvier. Rico Figueroa. Koji Yagano. They're the other ones going on this trip?"

Flint nodded. "Hall is Australian, Bouvier is French, Figueroa from Argentina and Yagano from Japan. Each writes freelance articles for men's travel-outdoor-adventure magazines in his own country."

"Then there's me, from the USA. The group is a veritable United Nations of travel magazines." Ashlinn managed a faint smile.

"And Paradise Outdoors will get advertising and publicity in all those magazines. This trip of Carmody's really was a good idea, and getting *Tour & Travel* to finance the whole thing took extraordinary salesmanship." Flint's irritation with his injured marketing chief appeared to soften.

"My entire staff is committed to taking the company into the global marketplace. I don't know how much you know about Paradise Outdoors, but we've grown from a small niche company selling specialized travel gear by catalog to a broader inventory and national customer base. Now we're headed worldwide." Flint's face lighted with enthusiasm as he talked about his company. Ashlinn found herself studying him, and as she watched and listened, her fear was transformed into something else entirely. All of a sudden, she was excruciatingly aware of everything about him.

Like his height. He literally towered over her, and in her boots with their three-inch heels, she was nearly five-eight, which wasn't exactly short.

He was strong too; he'd proven that by whisking along her ten-ton suitcases like feather pillows. The short sleeves of his white cotton shirt revealed the hard muscles of his arms.

Ashlinn swallowed hard. He was tall and strong—and then there was the additional matter of his looks. Somehow, those hadn't registered until now, either. He was *very* handsome, not to mention virile-looking.

Her mouth was dry. "Tall, dark, and handsome" was a cliché, but definitely applied to him. Words were her stock-in-trade, and Ashlinn realized she could come up with a thesaurus-full to describe Flint Paradise.

He seemed to be expecting some response from her. Floundering in the mind-shattering seas of sexual awareness, Ashlinn couldn't think of a single thing to say.

"My father started the business thirty years ago, and I took over as CEO after his death seven years ago. My staff instituted the full-color catalog, expanded the inventory and the mailing list and got a website on the Internet for cybersales. We're well situated to take Paradise Outdoors into the millennium,'' Flint proudly volunteered, with no prompting from her.

"Paradise is an unusual name, a good one for your company,'' Ashlinn finally came up with something to say, but she winced upon hearing it aloud. Could that really be her? She sounded like a simp! Self-consciousness struck, accompanied by an adrenaline rush. Mature women of twenty-eight did not develop instant crushes, did they? Yet she was behaving as if that was exactly what had just happened to her.

Thank heavens Flint seemed unaware of it.

"We were told our great-grandfather chose the name *Paradise*,'' he explained. "The chief was a Lakota Sioux and liked the sound of that particular Anglo word, so he decided to use it for his name.''

Flint's eyes locked with Ashlinn's.

"Lakota Sioux? Like in *Dances with Wolves*?''

"Yeah.'' Flint gave a laugh. "I keep forgetting about that movie, but people, especially women, keep reminding me.''

Ashlinn suspected he was laughing at her but carried on anyway. "There's a certain chic to being Native American,'' she suggested.

Not to mention romance, added a teasing little voice in her head. And he does conjure up thoughts of romance, doesn't he?

She couldn't seem to tear her gaze away from Flint Paradise. He had a long straight nose, high cheekbones, a well-shaped mouth and his skin was the color of polished bronze. He really did bear a resemblance to a hero on the cover of an historical romance novel—not that she read them, she preferred her history straight and factual, not plagued by love. There were a few key differences, of course. Flint's thick glossy black hair was cut short, and she was fairly certain that the male cover models wore theirs long and untamed. And Flint's white designer polo shirt and khaki trousers were a far cry from the loin cloths and feathers favored on the book covers.

"Dad was Sioux and Mom was Irish," Flint recited his bloodlines with a nonchalant shrug. "And my brother and sister and I prefer the term *Indian* to *Native American*. Just a personal preference, not a political statement either way."

She nodded her head, gazing into eyes that were almond-shaped and black as coal. When he looked at her the way he was doing now, his heated gaze seemed to liquefy her insides.

"We have to get going," he said, reaching out to touch her arm. "Get in."

For a moment, he thought she was going to balk, to refuse and run back into the airport terminal.

It would be for the best if she did, he decided, because just standing here looking at her during this time-filling, time-wasting conversation was turning him on so fast and so hard that the prospect of spending additional time with her, of sharing a tent with her...

That stunning realization struck him for the first time. The six men booked for the trip were to sleep in pairs in three tents. Hall was matched with Yagano, Bouvier with Figueroa, Sam Carmody with Asher Carey.

Which meant that Flint Paradise was assigned a tent with Ashlinn Carey! He was supposed to sleep in closest proximity to her for the next two weeks!

Flint removed his hand at the same moment she jumped back. He could still feel the softness of her skin under his palm, and he robotically flexed his fingers. That he had touched her at all was uncharacteristic of him. He wasn't the touchy-feely sort, given to casual physical contact. Yet he'd reached out and taken Ashlinn by the arm, which practically qualified as an intimate act for him! Such behavior was way out of line, Flint reproved himself. After all, the arrangement between *Tour & Travel* magazine and Paradise Outdoors made them colleagues, professionals working together.

But then, she was supposed to be Asher Carey, a red-blooded man's man, not Ashlinn, an irresistible temptress.

They couldn't go on this trip together. It was as simple as that. Now, all he had to do was to tell her so, to cancel the entire excursion and reimburse *Tour & Travel* and the other four members of the expedition.

Ashlinn moistened her lips. His touch seemed to be seared onto her skin like a brand. She could still feel the warmth and strength of his big hand. She couldn't stay, she decided. Not when she felt this forceful attraction to Flint Paradise. It was both scary and thrilling, like being on a roller coaster heading toward the top of a precipitous drop at warp speed.

Ashlinn had always hated roller coasters.

She would tell him that she was leaving Sioux Falls, that she was going back into the terminal right now, and no, he needn't bother to help her carry her suitcases back inside, thanks very much. She was going to fly back to New York tonight if she had to go by way of Seattle to do so.

But despite the decisive plans being concocted in their heads, neither Flint nor Ashlinn spoke a word.

Flint continued to hold the door for her, and she slipped into the front seat of the car, watching as he walked around to the driver's side and climbed inside.

Both simultaneously buckled their seatbelts. The clicks of the metal clasps were the only sounds heard within the confines of the car.

Flint turned the ignition key and the engine kicked into gear.

They were on their way.

Two

"**E**arlier this evening, I got the key to your motel room and put some of your new Paradise Outdoors gear in there," Flint said at last, breaking the silence between them.

It was rare for him to take the lead in making conversation, but he felt that need now. Ashlinn's presence was galvanizing.

"You have the key to my room?"

He could guess what she must think. "I didn't keep it, of course. I turned it back in at the desk," he assured her hastily.

Suddenly a vivid erotic fantasy flashed to mind, featuring himself slipping the key into the lock and entering her room where she waited for him in the darkness, lying on the bed wearing nothing but a drowsy, welcoming smile.

Flint coughed and gave his head a quick shake. Luckily, his mind cleared.

"You'll have to repack, using our extended-journey backpack." It was a command, not a suggestion.

"You actually expect me to take two weeks' worth of

clothes and supplies from my two full-size suitcases and stuff
it all into a backpack?'' Ashlinn sounded edgy and incredulous.

But she was glad they were talking again. Sitting in total
silence while the car whizzed along the interstate highway left
her too much time to imagine what lay ahead. Already a nervous anticipation was building within her.

"Yes, I actually expect you to do that, Ashlinn."

The sound of her name on his lips stunned her back into
silence.

It was stupid to get so rattled because he'd simply called her
by her own name, Ashlinn admonished herself. Except calling
her by name made things between them seem *personal.*

And of course, there was nothing personal between them;
there was absolutely nothing between them at all. This foolish
crush she seemed to have developed on him was certainly one-
sided and didn't count. She'd better quash it fast, before she
truly humiliated herself.

"Where will I keep my suitcases and the things left behind
in them?'' Ashlinn was pleased that her voice sounded crisp
and efficient, no small feat when she still felt like a dazed
schoolgirl. "Do I have the hotel room for the full two weeks?"

It seemed a possibility at this point. With *Tour & Travel*
financing the entire expedition, further extravagance on Junior's part wouldn't surprise her at all.

"Junior isn't *that* much of a spendthrift. Not when he's not
the recipient of his own largesse.''

Ashlinn looked over at Flint, startled. It was as if he'd read
her mind.

They traded brief spontaneous smiles, then swiftly, rather
guiltily, reset their frowns.

"You can leave the rest of your belongings in my office at
company headquarters," Flint said stiffly. "We'll have to head
there first tomorrow morning to get you fitted with hiking boots
and some special socks and, uh," he cleared his throat. "A
few personal things the catalog carries, things that are specifically sized and designed for women."

"First? You don't mean we're going there *before* dawn, do you?"

"We have to. The other guys already have everything and will expect to leave on schedule. They arrived this afternoon, as Carmody advised everybody to do. You're the only member of the group who insisted on taking a late flight in."

"I didn't insist. I was told the departure time and handed a ticket. And now I've got an assignment to complete, if I want to keep my job."

She turned toward him. "Will you help me do that, Flint?"

It was the first time she'd said his name and the effect upon Flint was hot and instant. He shifted uncomfortably and hoped she wasn't looking at his lap because his body wasn't keeping any secret of his attraction to her. It responded reflexively, despite his attempt to will otherwise.

"I'll—do what I can," he mumbled, forbidding his eyes to look her way. He trained his gaze ahead, on the monotonous flow of traffic on the interstate.

"Good. Thank you. The first thing we need is to bring some other women along on this trip," Ashlinn said briskly.

Flint tensed. She'd wrung a simple note of compliance from him, and already she was giving orders. She thought all she had to do was to whisper his name and he'd melt like a snowball in July. Well, Ashlinn Carey was in for a surprise. His sobriquet, "Iceman," had been deservedly earned. He didn't melt for anyone.

"More women? You want to make this trip into some kind of Beach Blanket Black Hills?" His voice lowered, his tone both cold and fierce. "Forget it, Ashlinn."

This time she wasn't charmed by his use of her name. "Do you really think I'm advocating some kind of Naked Singles romp in the great outdoors? Ha, you wish! All I mean is that we need more women on this trip to curb the bouts of macho male bonding and competition. You know they're bound to occur."

"I don't know what you're talking about," snapped Flint. "I wonder if you do."

"I certainly do. I know that one woman among five men is practically a nonentity. The five of you will forge ahead without me, you'll do things I simply can't. I know how guys act, I have an older brother and two stepbrothers. And I also know that having a balanced number of women in a group sets a different tone. The presence of women provides certain guidelines and constraints and limits to the…"

"You're imparting the viewpoint of women-as-the-old-ball-and-chain? Interesting."

"Of course, should you guys still insist on jumping off cliffs or swimming in hypothermia-inducing water, at least I'll have some company picking berries while you're doing it."

Flint smirked. "Who would have thought a sophisticated big-city lady editor would attest to the stereotypes of action-oriented, risk-taking male and passive berry-picking female?"

"Who would have thought?" she echoed, not rising to the bait. "Will you call some women you know and ask them to come with us?"

"We leave tomorrow at dawn, remember? That's not enough notice. Nobody can just pick up and leave so quickly."

"You could at least *try*. Call your girlfriend. Won't she jump at the chance to spend the next two weeks with you?"

Ashlinn attempted to ignore the flush that suffused her face and spread throughout her whole body. She wasn't fishing for information, she assured herself; she was merely confirming the inevitable. Odds were great that a man like Flint Paradise—handsome and successful—did have a girlfriend. Maybe several.

"I don't have a girlfriend," Flint said bluntly.

A swell of joy surged through her followed by a rush of embarrassment. If he were to guess…

Ashlinn shuddered. "Then call some of the women, uh, you date casually," she strove to sound blasé.

"I don't date," Flint growled through his teeth. "I don't have the time for it. My work is my life. Paradise Outdoors is all I want and need. Is that so difficult to understand?"

Her eyes widened. "I get the feeling you've had this conversation before—with somebody who puts you very much on the defensive.''

''I'm not on the defen—'' he abruptly paused, then breathed a sigh. ''Okay, maybe I am, a little.''

''Who nags you about working too much and too hard?'' Ashlinn pressed, curious. ''Your parents? Mine accuse me of being too dedicated to my career. They have a 'you're letting life pass you by' speech that I can recite word for word. I hear it almost every Sunday during our weekly phone calls.''

''My folks are both dead, so no, they don't worry about my lack of a social life.''

''I'm sorry about your parents. Has to be a sister, then. I know how sisters are, I have a younger one plus two stepsisters.''

''My sister is in her senior year in medical school, and she's as devoted to her work as I am to mine. No, Eva would never nag me, but my brother has been known to make some pointed comments about my priorities.''

''Brothers can be just as interfering as sisters,'' Ashlinn conceded.

Flint angled a quick look at her.

A shaft of moonlight cast her delicate profile in relief. Stop it! he admonished himself. Think of her as a customer, not a lovely desirable woman. Pretend she is *Asher* Carey and make trivial conversation. Become bored, immediately!

''You already mentioned a slew of brothers.'' Listening to anyone drone on about their family normally had a narcotic effect upon him. Surely it would be no different with her, no matter how sexy she was. ''How big is your family anyway?''

''Big. We're a Brady Bunch-type clan. My mom had three kids when she married my stepdad, who had four.''

''Now *there's* a prescription for disaster!'' Flint exclaimed. Unfortunately, being startled and appalled was the antithesis of boredom.

Ashlinn looked at him in surprise. ''What makes you say that?''

"Because it's so obvious. Keep in mind the Bradys are *fictional* characters, Ashlinn. In real life…"

"Things worked out well," Ashlinn cut in. "The seven of us are all grown up and on our own and the folks are happily retired in Florida. See, a fairy-tale ending."

"I don't like fairy tales," Flint growled. "Never have. I can't suspend the disbelief."

"How about sociology, then? The Careys are a successful case of a modern blended family."

"Even fairy tales are more believable than that."

"You couldn't be this negative on the subject unless you've had some personal involvement with it." Her interest was piqued. "Were you married to a woman with kids who…"

"God, no!" His invocation of the Almighty was heartfelt. "I have never been married, nor do I intend to be. The whole point of marriage is to have a family and I already have more family than I know what to do with. The last thing I need or want is any more relatives."

His vehemence amused her. "Who's the worst?"

"Are you taking about relatives?"

She nodded. "If my family were polled, I'm sure *I'd* win the title of The Worst One. I was an overly dramatic child and a sarcastic, bratty teen. I like to think I've improved as an adult, but I'm afraid that among my relatives, my reputation is set in cement."

"Your family has yet to experience the worst," Flint assured her. "My two half sisters hold the Worldwide Worst title. Of course, their late unlamented mother made Lucrezia Borgia look like a real sweetheart, so they come by it naturally, I suppose."

"If their black-hearted mom wasn't yours too, that means you shared the same father," Ashlinn surmised easily.

"Yes, Ben Paradise." Flint's black eyes were hard. "A year after my mother's death, Dad married Marcine, who spawned Camryn and Kaylin."

"Sounds like you're still holding a grudge against her for that."

"Among other things. And after observing my father's misery with Marcine, I have no desire to experience the gothic horror known as marriage first-hand."

Ashlinn wasn't sure if she ought to offer a counterargument. Emphasizing the success of her family seemed insensitive at best, boastful at worst, when Flint's own fell into the dysfunctional category.

They both lapsed into a silence which soon grew oppressive to Ashlinn.

"Now that you're all adults, do you ever see your half sisters?" she asked. She knew how easy it would be to sever family ties as an adult; she had to make a special effort to keep in touch with her own siblings and steps, who were scattered all over the country. She did it willingly. But then, she didn't consider any of them to be satanic spawns. Hopefully, they no longer saw her as one.

"Camryn and Kaylin aren't adults, they're teenagers and live with my brother here in town." His tone was dour. "So I see them."

"They're in Sioux Falls?" An idea, born of desperation, suddenly dawned on her. "We could ask *them* to come camping with us tomorrow!"

"Have you heard a word I said?" Flint was astounded. "Why in the world would I take those two hellions camping? I wouldn't take them anywhere! I can barely make it through an occasional dinner at my brother's home with them, let alone two full weeks of..."

"But we need more females on the trip, and you haven't come up with anybody else. Anyway, chances are better for teens to be able to go somewhere at the last minute than for..."

"Absolutely not!" Flint cut in again. "If you knew Camryn and Kaylin, you would realize how truly terrible your idea really is."

"Introduce me to them," Ashlinn said boldly. "If they're as bad as you say, then obviously, I won't want them along. But if you're harboring some kind of grudge against two perfectly normal kids just because you didn't like their mother marrying your father, then I want them on the trip.''

''Lady, if you're trying to infuriate me, you've succeeded beyond your wildest expectations!''

''I'm beginning to believe I'm on the right track,'' countered Ashlinn. ''After all, they live with your brother. He must like them, so how awful can they be? Unless you can't stand your brother, either?''

''I love my brother!'' Flint declared with a fervor that touched her. ''But unfortunately, he has an exaggerated sense of duty. In fact, Rafe is probably the most dutiful person on the planet. He took in the girls after their mother died three years ago and kept them, even though they've wreaked havoc on his life.''

''Hmm,'' said Ashlinn.

''You don't believe me?'' Flint was indignant. ''Okay, I'll let you be the judge. I'll take you to Rafe's house and you can meet the girls. One minute in their company will have you convinced beyond a shadow of a doubt that you don't want to spend another one. They're all night owls, so we can just drop in.''

His tone was so ominous that Ashlinn felt more than a little apprehensive. Did she really want to meet two bad seeds? She buoyed her courage by thinking of Junior, the boy boss. If she could endure working for *him* day after day, taking a few minutes to assess Flint's allegedly demonic half sisters would be a breeze.

Flint was heartily regretting his rash challenge by the time he turned onto Deer Trail Lane, a tree-lined street in a well-tended housing development. Bringing Ashlinn here was stupid beyond imagining, but since he'd let her goad him into it, he could only blame himself. His jaw clenched.

''This is a nice neighborhood,'' Ashlinn remarked politely as they drove along the long street.

''My brother used to own half a duplex farther down this road, but he bought a single-family house a few months ago.

Seems like he's always working on the place. His latest project is to convert the garage into an extra room.''

Flint sighed wistfully, remembering better days, when Rafe had plenty of spare time to spend with him and Eva. Not anymore. It had been months since the three of them had gone out to dinner together or taken in a movie.

"I'm assuming he got a bigger place because of the half sisters you can't stand?" Ashlinn couldn't resist mentioning the obvious.

"Not just for them," Flint protested halfheartedly. "Rafe got married last Thanksgiving and his wife wanted more room too." He pulled into the double driveway of a big two-story house. "In addition to the girls, they have two foster kids, little boys, Trent and Tony."

"They've only been married for about eight months and they have four kids living with them?" Ashlinn was impressed. "Your brother sounds wonderful, a guy like my stepdad. It takes a very special kind of man to share his life and his wife, especially with kids who aren't his own."

"Yeah." Flint, who truly loved and admired his brother, felt an ignoble rivalrous niggling as she rhapsodized about Rafe, which was odd, because he was always the one to lead the chorus of praise for Rafe. It was unnerving to consider the possibility that he wanted to hear Ashlinn rave about *Flint* Paradise. Unnerving and alarming as hell!

And worse was yet to come.

Ashlinn was out of the car and halfway to the front door of the house when she noticed that Flint was lagging behind. Quite purposefully, it seemed to her.

"A prisoner on his way to the electric chair probably keeps the same pace you're doing right now," she observed dryly, pausing to wait for him to catch up to her.

"I probably should warn you." Flint cleared his throat.

He arrived to stand beside her, not realizing how closely until their shoulders brushed. It was unlike him to invade someone's personal space; he normally kept a definitive distance between himself and another. Not this time. When he turned slightly, the entire length of their arms were touching, and his hand skimmed hers.

But Ashlinn made no move away from him. "About what?" she murmured.

Flint remained where he was. He inhaled deeply, and the aroma of her shampoo, a tantalizing spicy scent, filled his nostrils. He fixed his eyes on her glossy black hair that looked so soft and silky it took considerable restraint to keep himself from touching it. Stroking it.

"I guess I should warn you that this might prove to be awkward in more ways than one." His voice lowered. "You see, there is—something of a strain between Rafe's wife, Holly, and me."

Ashlinn looked up at him, her dark eyes illuminated in the bright porch-lights. "Is it her fault? Or yours?"

He was instantly annoyed. "If you're looking to incriminate someone, don't choose Holly. She isn't to blame for anything. I'm the one at fault." He strode toward the door, his head held high and proud.

"I wasn't trying to incriminate anybody." Ashlinn scurried after him. "I was just trying to get a better handle on the situation."

They reached the small porch. She stumbled as her heel caught on the top step, and automatically, Flint reached out to catch hold of her waist, steadying her. Ashlinn laid her hands on his forearms, bracing herself.

She lifted her head and their eyes met. Their position was not unlike that of a couple on the verge of a kiss, in those first early uncertain seconds of contact before moving into each other's arms.

Ashlinn's heartbeat seemed to echo in her ears. "Thanks. I—I've been warned that the heels on these boots will end up killing me."

"They aren't at all practical." Flint frowned his disapproval. "Paradise Outdoors would never carry such useless merchandise. Luckily, you'll get a much better, *functional* pair of boots tomorrow."

His fingers tightened briefly on the curve of her waist, then he dropped his hands and stepped away from her, out of touching range.

She could feel the phantom pressure of his hands on her. Ashlinn told herself she wasn't disappointed, she was *relieved* he hadn't tried to kiss her. She wouldn't have allowed him, of course; after all, she hardly knew him.

But he hadn't even tried…

"You were about to tell me about the—the strain between you and your sister-in-law," she reminded him.

Her body was still pulsing with the urgency he'd roused—and left unslaked. Had he been affected by their proximity at all? she wondered. Since he'd half turned away from her, she couldn't clearly observe him. Yet he seemed calm enough. *She* was the one whose breathing was closer to panting.

Ashlinn looked away from him, forcing herself to study the decorative grapevine wreath on the front door. Red, white and blue ribbons were woven through it, presumably in homage to last week's Fourth of July holiday.

"About Holly…" Flint was struggling with his own urgency and control.

What better way to quell desire than to remember how wrong he'd been about Holly? If he were ever asked to cite his turn-offs, being wrong would head the list.

"I made the drastic mistake of jumping to all the wrong conclusions about Holly when my brother first got involved with her," he said dolefully. "Unfortunately, I shared my opinions with Rafe and strongly advised him against marrying her."

"Been there." Ashlinn gave a rueful sigh. "Done that— *twice.* I zealously warned both my sister Courtney and my stepsister Michelle not to get involved with the men they ended up marrying."

"Twice?" repeated Flint.

"I didn't learn from my mistake the first time." Ashlinn did not spare herself. "I didn't let Courtney's marital success keep me from insisting that Michelle was doomed to misery. I bet if Eva started dating someone seriously, you'd think long and hard about shoving your negative opinions down her throat.''

''Yes,'' agreed Flint. ''I certainly would.'' He couldn't envision himself making the same mistake twice.

A peculiar sense of relief was surging through him. His gross misjudgment of Holly continued to plague him, but hearing that Ashlinn had fallen prey to similar errors *twice* was oddly heartening.

''I told Rafe that Holly was a calculating manipulator,'' he dared to confess.

Ashlinn remained unshocked. ''I told Courtney and Michelle that Connor and Steve were insincere users, the kind of smooth operators who would dump them and break their hearts. And both guys turned out to be model husbands and fathers, devoted to their wives and children. My stepbrother said I was a sour pessimist and my own brother told me I was jealous of Courtney and Michelle.'' She winced.

''Why don't people appreciate good old-fashioned caution these days? Just try to exercise it, and others completely misunderstand your motives!'' Flint was incensed on her behalf. ''I've only spent a short time with you, but I can certainly tell that you're neither sour nor pessimistic.''

''Thanks,'' murmured Ashlinn. ''I'm not jealous of Courtney and Michelle either. Honest.''

''I believe you.'' He took a deep breath. ''I originally saw Holly as a schemer with an agenda and thought it was my brotherly obligation to tell Rafe what he was up against.''

''Let me guess what happened,'' Ashlinn said wryly. ''Holly turned out to be the ideal wife for your brother.''

''She turned out to be a *saint!*''

Ashlinn smiled at the hyperbole. ''You have to be dead to be a saint, Flint, that's the rule.''

''Well, Holly is a living saint,'' Flint insisted. ''She's a doctor, a psychiatrist who's established a solid practice and is respected and admired by the medical community here. Even more important, she's made my brother happier than I've ever seen him. *And* she's committed to those four impossible kids who aren't even hers."

"She does sound like a paragon. Seems like you and I have both proven how perceptive we are when it comes to love and romance," Ashlinn said lightly. "Which is to say, not at all. We're definitely better off dedicating our energy to our careers."

"Yes." Flint nodded his agreement. "But I have to admit that hearing you made the same mistake I did—twice—makes me feel less like a paranoid lunatic."

Her dark eyes gleamed. "If I'm not a sour jealous pessimist, you certainly aren't a paranoid lunatic."

They stared at each other, their expressions conveying mutual understanding, mutual acceptance. Both took an unconscious step closer.

"Eewww! Look who's lurking around our house!" A piercing young voice sharply broke the aura of intimacy enveloping them. Seemingly from nowhere, a Jeep Cherokee had appeared, and emanating from it was that girlish voice of pure disdain.

Flint and Ashlinn jumped apart, almost to opposite ends of the small porch. The vehicle came to a screeching halt in the driveway, the doors were flung open, and two dark-haired girls jumped out.

Ashlinn didn't have to ask who they were. Flint's face was dark as a thundercloud as he watched his two teenaged half sisters saunter to the door, their young faces surly as they stared from him to Ashlinn.

"Make sure you get your cash from him upfront, honey," one girl addressed Ashlinn, her tone and her dark eyes insolent. "And I hope you're up to date on your shots, especially your rabies shot."

The other one snickered.

"You can apologize to Miss Carey right now, Camryn," snapped Flint. "And you too, Kaylin."

"'Cause you told us to?" Camryn laughed. "Yeah, right. That'll happen."

She brushed by Ashlinn and Flint and entered the house, her younger sister close on her heels.

Flint automatically moved to follow them inside. The door slammed shut.

"Well, now you've met them," he growled. "Was I exaggerating?"

"I've never seen a door literally slammed in someone's face before," Ashlinn said uneasily. "Do they do that often?"

He didn't bother to answer. "Come on, let's get out of here."

Ashlinn wasn't about to argue. The teenagers couldn't have made it more clear that she and Flint were unwelcome. And just like he'd said, taking them camping was out of the question. But just as the two turned to leave, the door opened again.

"The girls said you were here, Flint. With a, er, a friend."

Ashlinn gaped at the man standing in the doorway, whose voice sounded exactly like Flint's. He looked exactly like Flint, too.

She stared from one brother to the other. If she didn't know that Flint was wearing the white shirt and khaki trousers, she wouldn't have been able to distinguish him from the other man, who wore a pair of faded old jeans and no shirt at all. His bare bronze chest shone in the light.

"You're twins!" she exclaimed, then grinned, unable not to. "I do have a remarkable grasp of the obvious, don't I?"

"I'm Rafe Paradise." He extended his hand to her to shake.

She took it and introduced herself while scrutinizing Rafe closely. The resemblance to Flint was uncanny, but on closer inspection, she noticed a few subtle differences. Rafe's face was more open, his expression friendlier in comparison to Flint, who appeared more guarded and aloof. Rafe's smiles came more easily; she already knew that Flint's were rare.

Rare and thrilling, she mused, remembering the potent impact Flint's smiles had upon her. But Flint was not smiling now.

"We were just leaving, Rafe," Flint said tersely. "Sorry to have disturbed you this late."

"It's my fault," Ashlinn interjected. "I was the one who insisted on coming."

Rafe didn't ask why. "Glad you're here. Come in." He cupped Ashlinn's elbow and ushered her inside, giving her no choice but to accept his invitation. Which gave Flint no choice but to follow them both into the house.

"Holly, we have company," Rafe called up the stairs.

"The evil twin's out of his crypt again," announced Camryn who stood on the stairway, eyeing Flint and Ashlinn. "And he brought the queen of Darkness with him."

"Be quiet, Camryn!" snapped Flint.

"Camryn, go to your room." Rafe heaved a sigh. "Now."

"You don't have to ask me twice!" Camryn flounced up the stairs.

"I know that little brat thinks she has a genetic right to insult me, but Ashlinn should not have to put up with it!" Flint, standing behind Ashlinn, placed a protective hand on her shoulder. His fingers tightened, drawing her back a little toward him.

"What's going on?"

Ashlinn turned at the sound and was sure that the tall slim brunette gliding regally down the stairs just had to be Holly, Rafe's wife. She studied the other woman. Flint had neglected to mention how beautiful his sister-in-law, the doctor, was.

Both Flint and Ashlinn stared at Holly, who was tying a knot in the navy silk belt that matched her robe. Her cheeks were flushed, her brown curls tousled. And then there was Rafe wearing only his—hastily pulled on?—jeans.

Ashlinn gulped. It did look as if they had intruded on a private moment between the couple. "We're so sorry to disturb you."

Holly and Rafe exchanged quick glances. "We were just watching a movie on TV," Holly said smoothly and introduced herself to Ashlinn.

"I guess you're wondering why we're here," Flint spoke up. "Ashlinn wanted to know if Camryn and Kaylin could come along on the Paradise Outdoors camping expedition, the one Carmody set up before his skateboard accident."

Rafe gaped, dumbfounded. "You want *them* to join you and your girlfriend on..."

"She is not my girlfriend!" Flint said vehemently, lifting his hand from Ashlinn's shoulder as if he'd been scalded. He immediately moved to stand apart from her.

Ashlinn tried to ignore her discomfort. "Can the girls come along?"

"Did you know that Camryn and her friends taught Sam Carmody how to skateboard?" Rafe frowned pensively. "We didn't like him hanging around with high-school kids and told her to stay away from him. Whether or not she listened is a..."

"The girls both have their jobs at the mall," Holly inserted. "They really can't leave on such short notice, Flint."

"So you two are going camping together?" Rafe arched his brows, his expression speculative as he studied Flint and Ashlinn. "Should be an interesting trip. Will you be sharing a tent?" he added, his eyes gleaming, unable to hold back from a little brotherly ribbing.

"It wasn't planned, it just worked out that way!" Flint was immediately defensive. A flush stained his cheeks, turning his skin a deep golden bronze. "This is ridiculous." He snatched Ashlinn's hand and pushed open the front door. "We're out of here, right now!" He left the house, dragging Ashlinn along with him.

They got into the car and sped away from the house.

"It wasn't planned, it just worked out that way?" Ashlinn repeated. Her heart began to pound, fast and loud. "Does that mean I'm actually supposed to share a tent with you?"

"You look panicked at the thought. Fearing for your virtue? Have you bought into Camryn's evil twin accusations?"

"I'm not panicked and I don't think you're evil, but I'm not sharing a tent with you or anyone else. I want my own tent! Since *Tour & Travel* is paying the expenses, just bill them for an extra tent. Because I will not..."

"Relax. I don't want to share a tent with you either. Asher Carey and I were assigned to share one, but Ms. Ashlinn Carey is definitely getting her own. The extra cost can come out of Junior's lunch money.''

"You were only joking." Ashlinn tucked a loose strand of hair behind her ear. Her hand was trembling. "I knew that."

"No, you didn't." He was clearly relishing her overreaction. "And I warned you the Paradise clan wasn't one big happy extended family like yours, but you insisted on meeting the girls. Well, I was right, wasn't I?" Flint's voice held an unmistakable ring of triumph.

"Are you one of those annoying types who always have to have the last word?"

"I'm not annoying, but yes, I've been told that I do like to have the last word," he admitted, not at all offended by the charge.

"Ohhhh! These next two weeks are going to be interminable." Ashlinn was vexed, but more with herself than with him. For there was an unwelcome excitement bubbling inside her that she couldn't suppress.

"Interminable," Flint agreed.

But his grim pronouncement was at odds with the slow smile playing across his face.

Three

By the time the Paradise Outdoors expedition arrived in Custer State Park the next afternoon, Ashlinn was uncomfortably aware that she had more in common with Presley Oakes Jr. than with her fellow campers. At least the boy publisher enjoyed city life and had never escaped from a war zone or attempted to climb Mount Everest.

Jack Hall, Etienne Bouvier, Rico Figueroa and Koji Yagano had done all that and much more. They were professional outdoorsmen and adventurers, each with a long resumé of successful feats and scrapes with death. In addition to writing about their escapades for their respective magazines, all four were proud contributors to *The Most Dangerous Places on the Globe,* a book Ashlinn had never heard of.

Flint had.

''The title is self-explanatory. It's a kind of guidebook for the most dangerous places in the world, destinations that aren't recommended for travelers,'' he explained as he drove the party in an enormous rented van to the park in southwestern South

Dakota. Ashlinn was sitting beside him in the front while the other four men sprawled two to a bench in back.

"They are places that definitely aren't recommended for tourists," added Jack Hall, his tone and expression making it clear that he considered tourists a threat to the quality of life, much the same as flesh-eating bacteria.

"Your state department forbids you to go to many of the places we've been," Rico Figueroa added enthusiastically.

"Then why go? And why bother with a guidebook for unsafe places?" Ashlinn asked what she considered to be the most obvious questions.

She heard a groan. An impatient sigh. And then silence descended.

Ashlinn chewed her lower lip. She'd done it again; it seemed she had a talent for exasperating this crew.

She cast a glance at Flint. At least he didn't look exasperated.

Flint caught her eye. "Maybe 'guidebook' isn't the best choice of word. Think reference book instead."

He'd responded politely to all her questions and remarks when the others wouldn't, Ashlinn mused gratefully.

"The book is more of an anthology," Flint continued, filling the silence. "The various contributors write about what they saw and did in dangerous cities and countries all over the world. There are plenty of armchair adventurers who enjoy experiencing danger vicariously."

"You're in travel publishing, Ashley, you know that," chided Jack Hall.

"It's Ashlinn," she corrected, not for the first time. "And *Tour & Travel* features articles on places like Sausalito and Williamsburg. Our readers want amenities and charm, not threats to their lives."

"But your new publisher is set on changing that," Flint reminded her.

As if she needed reminding! Ashlinn sighed.

"Custer State Park probably is less dangerous than crossing any street in Paris, but our stay there will be a useful respite," said Etienne Bouvier. "With no distractions in the evenings, I plan to polish my article on my encounter with headhunters."

"Before you ask," Flint murmured under his breath to Ashlinn. "He's not referring to an executive search agency."

She knew he was kidding and chuckled quietly. "I think they'd throw me out of the van if I asked, even as a joke," she whispered back. "They take their adventures very seriously."

"The next two weeks are the equivalent of lying in the sun on a beach, something I rarely do," piped up Rico. "But I intend to completely relax on this trip."

"We're scheduled to rock climb, mountain bike and climb a peak, among other activities," Ashlinn pointed out, reciting their proposed itinerary from the list she'd been given that morning. "None of that can be termed relaxing."

For her, just thinking of what lay ahead was fatigue-inducing. The possibility of relaxation during the next two weeks seemed as remote as their campsite.

"I think that climbing Harney Peak, which is 7,242 feet high, might qualify as relaxation compared to the twenty-thousand-some feet they scaled on Everest," observed Flint.

"I guess when you put it like that…" Ashlinn's voice trailed off.

The thought of attempting to climb over seven thousand feet still did not strike her as child's play. She pictured rocks and falls and broken bones.

"Glad you're along to translate for the lady, Flint," Koji said gratefully.

Ashlinn knew he wasn't referring to language difficulties, because all the men spoke English fluently. Nor was the lack of understanding between her and her fellow campers the result of typical male/female differences so well-documented in the pop psychology books proliferating on bookstore shelves.

No, she and the four international risk takers were like creatures from separate universes with absolutely no common frame of reference. She found their bold mindset, their casual bravado, so incomprehensible that even small talk posed a difficulty. Since they'd met this morning, she'd invariably said the wrong thing, irking or boring the four happy wanderers.

But as Koji had mentioned, Flint was proving valuable as a translator cum peacemaker, interpreting her to the men and vice versa. Though he hadn't risked his life on seven continents, somehow, fortunately, he was able to relate both to those who had and to Ashlinn.

"Since she's offering no fringe benefits, we're grateful you don't mind baby-sitting her, Flint," said Jack Hall in a relieved better-you-than-me tone.

Ashlinn couldn't let that remark go unchallenged. "That crack about fringe benefits is too low to dignify with a rejoinder, and I don't need a baby-sitter!"

The four men laughed, as if she'd told a hilarious joke.

"You need a baby-sitter a helluva lot more than we need a guide, *chica*," said Rico. "The four of us have had more than enough experience to be on our own in a state park in South Dakota. You can't say the same."

More hearty macho laughter. More stories of being held at gunpoint, of drinking snake blood, of bribing their way in and out of the hellholes of the world while loving every minute of it.

Ashlinn leaned her head against the window and closed her eyes, pretending she'd nodded off to sleep. She had already had enough interaction with her campmates. Two whole weeks with them loomed like an eternity.

It seemed ironic that last night, she had been apprehensive about spending the next two weeks with Flint. Who could have guessed that today she would consider him the closest thing she had to a friend and ally?

But it was true. Flint was courteous, treating her as an equal member of the expedition, not an unwelcome pest. The same couldn't be said for the others in the group.

Ashlinn's mind drifted back to her meeting with them this morning, after her predawn trip to Paradise Outdoors' company headquarters with Flint. To the fateful moment when she'd informed the men that she not only wasn't a good cook, but her campfire cuisine was even worse than her everyday efforts.

"But cooking is what women are created for!" Rico exclaimed, shocked.

Ashlinn had felt obliged to offer a rebuttal. What woman wouldn't? But Flint had caught her hand, pulling her out of earshot of the group.

"For the sake of congeniality, I recommend just letting that one pass," he suggested quietly.

"But he just relegated women back to the Stone Age!" objected Ashlinn. "On behalf of women everywhere, I..."

"You can talk till you're hoarse, but you'll never convince him otherwise. Anyway, the men agreed to do the cooking for themselves," Flint pointed out. "You won't be slaving over a hot campfire, except to make your own meals. Can't you view that as a victory on behalf of women everywhere?"

"I guess so." Ashlinn was very aware that Flint was still holding her hand. A small shiver rippled along her spine.

"Cooking isn't the only thing women are good for," Bouvier had interjected, his eyes raking Ashlinn's trim blue-jeaned figure. "Don't forget about sex."

"As if we ever could!" Jack Hall had laughed rakishly. "Maybe you'll share your tent with one of us, lovely lady? Or all of us, if the gods are smiling."

Ashlinn didn't know if he was kidding or not but decided to set the record straight right from the beginning.

"The gods aren't smiling," she said succinctly. "So don't bother going through the motions, because you've already struck out."

Only Bouvier didn't get her baseball metaphor. "I have a can of Mace," Ashlinn clarified her position for him. "If you try anything with me, I'll use it on you."

"So you've already made your choice, then?" Koji's eyes were fixed on her hand linked with Flint's.

Her face flaming, Ashlinn dropped Flint's hand. "My choice is to be left alone!"

Just in case they decided to take her literally and abandon

her in the wild, she added, "I expect to be treated exactly like any other member of this group. As if I were *Asher* Carey."

Rico said something in a language she didn't recognize and they all laughed. Except Flint. He looked as uncomprehending as she did.

"An old Sinhalese saying," Koji explained. "Remind us to translate later, Flint."

Ashlinn guessed the remark was outrageously sexist and dealt with a woman's place in the most insulting terms. Well, she didn't want to be here any more than they wanted her along. It was just too bad she was so totally outnumbered. If only Flint's half sisters hadn't been so impossible.

As the four men swapped tales of the smugglers' bazaar in Peshawar, Ashlinn fell into a light fitful sleep that lasted until the van came to a stop.

She opened her eyes to see an enormous buffalo standing a few feet away, staring straight at her. She gasped.

"Bison," Flint laid his hand on her arm. "Don't be alarmed. There are about fourteen hundred of them roaming in the park. We're on Wildlife Loop Road, and they often stop traffic along this stretch."

Several cars were stopped behind them on the narrow road as a few bison meandered across. More animals were grazing on either side of the road.

"I've never seen a live buffalo before," she said, awed. "Only stuffed ones in museums."

"I'd like to ride one of those," enthused Jack Hall. "I've ridden camels in Saudi and elephants in India."

"Haven't we all?" Figueroa sounded bored.

Ashlinn and Flint caught each other's eye. "Camels and elephants are so passé," she imitated Figueroa's jaded tone. "Riding bison is the latest thrill."

Flint swallowed a smile. "Riding bison is forbidden," he informed his charges. "They can be dangerously unpredictable and bad-tempered."

"With this group, you're better off saying bison are so tame that even grandmothers find them dull to ride," Ashlinn murmured. "Nothing seems to excite our fellow campers more than the possibility of breaking every bone in their bodies."

Flint laughed.

"What's so funny?" demanded Bouvier.

"Ashlinn just made a—um—a buffalo joke," Flint said, as they exchanged conspiratorial smiles.

"Your ancestors worshipped the buffalo, didn't they, Flint?" Koji asked respectfully. "I've read a lot about the American Wild West."

Since Flint had made it clear he was a modern-day workaholic who preferred his office to anywhere else, the Wild West reference struck Ashlinn as particularly absurd. She couldn't stifle another outburst of laughter.

"Now you're laughing at Flint's native culture?" Bouvier's voice was icy with disapproval.

"No, of course not," she said quickly. "It's just that I can't picture Flint in the Old West era."

"I can," said Koji, and launched into an impassioned discourse about the softness of contemporary society and its toxic effect on men. Fortunately, according to him, the five men in the van were immune to this modern-day plague and remained true men's men; living, breathing tributes to the hardy male warriors who preceded them.

"I wasn't accusing you of being a couch potato," Ashlinn murmured to Flint. "Honest."

"I know," he replied, his voice equally low.

Not that it mattered, because the four warriors in the back weren't interested in the conversation going on in the front. They'd already launched into an eager discussion about the challenges of hunting for game in assorted trouble spots.

"Just for the record, I prefer contemporary times," continued Flint. "I'll take one of the Paradise Outdoors water-tight tents instead of a lean-to made out of sticks and mud any day."

"A cell phone over smoke signals," added Ashlinn.

Flint nodded. "A pair of Paradise Outdoors woodsman boots with Durotech socks rather than moccasins."

"Paradise Outdoors power-zoom binoculars instead of

squinting.'' She shrugged apologetically. ''I'm running out of examples, that was the best I could do.''

''There are countless examples,'' enthused Flint. ''Let's start with this GPS automotive navigator sold by Paradise Outdoors.''

He pointed to the electronic geopositional satellite unit mounted on the dash. ''The unit has built-in maps of highways and major metro streets in the United States and most of Canada and Mexico, and also includes rivers and lakes. It continuously tracks and uses up to twelve satellites for precise operations.''

Ashlinn was impressed. ''That makes a compass seem obsolete.''

''Although Paradise Outdoors does sell a wide range of fine compasses,'' Flint added quickly, never one to disparage any merchandise sold by his company.

''Maybe for nostalgia buffs?'' teased Ashlinn. ''How's that for a marketing hook?''

''Pretty bad, but I've heard worse,'' said Flint.

''Surely not from Skatin' Sam Carmody, marketing genius?'' Ashlinn suggested.

''Why are you so down on Carmody?'' Flint asked. ''Actually, I'd like to bring him into the family, convince him to try his luck with Eva.''

''Sam Carmody and Eva?'' quizzed Ashlinn.

Flint nodded his approval. ''Carmody and Eva would be good together. The company would get to keep a stellar marketing talent in the family and—er—''

''Yes, 'and—er,''' Ashlinn mocked. ''Paradise Outdoors would get to keep Carmody, but how would Eva benefit? What does she get out of such a setup?''

''Eva has stock in the company. What's good for Paradise Outdoors is good for every member of the Paradise family?'' suggested Flint. ''A fairly weak argument, I'll grant you that.''

''I should mention that family fix-ups and all the expectations that go with them usually bomb big time,'' Ashlinn warned. ''I'm speaking from personal experience.''

"Your family has tried to fix you up a lot?" Flint realized he was scowling. His gut began to churn when he also realized how much he absolutely hated the thought of her dating a lot of different men, family setups or not. He hated the thought of her dating *any* man.

His breath caught in his throat. Good Lord, he couldn't be jealous, not him. Flint Paradise had never succumbed to sexual jealousy in his life. And to feel jealous of the unnamed, unknown men who'd been set up with Ashlinn…that was foolish beyond reason. And he was infinitely reasonable, never foolish. He could only be relieved that she appeared to be completely unaware of his inner turmoil.

"Finding a match for me was turning into a regular Carey family project," Ashlinn replied, and heaved a groan. "But I finally had to lay down the law and tell them no more matchmaking, especially after the last guy."

"Bad?" asked Flint. He knew he sounded too hopeful and hoped she hadn't noticed.

She hadn't.

"Bad doesn't begin to cover it. Try 'unendurable.' I have my sister Courtney to thank for inflicting her brother-in-law Nathaniel Tremaine on me." Ashlinn shuddered at the memory.

"Can we assume you'd rather drink snake blood or be on the run from fanatic guerrillas than suffer through another date with him?" Flint pressed, growing ever more cheerful.

"Definitely! To call Nathaniel shallow is to give him undeserved depth. I threw such a fit after that disastrous weekend my family finally agreed they should drop the Cupid role and take my career as seriously as I do."

"So, your career really is the sole focus of your life. You don't have a…"

"If you say 'special someone,' I won't be responsible for my actions," cautioned Ashlinn.

"How about significant other, then?" Flint suggested lightly.

"Not one of those, either." She folded her arms in front of

her chest and stared straight ahead at the buffalo lumbering across the road.

No "special someone" or "significant other." Flint almost smiled. Almost. Then he realized how very unlike him it was to grill a woman about such things. And though he had pretty much concluded from their conversation last night that Ashlinn was unattached, suddenly he'd needed to hear absolute confirmation of her status from her own lips.

Her lips...he stole a quick glance at her mouth. Those sensuously full lips of hers were curved into a pout that struck him as both sultry and arousing. A streak of heat jolted through him.

Last night he'd had the most disturbing dream about her, about that sexy little mouth of hers moving over every inch of his skin. Then, just as she was about to take his most crucial inches between her lips, the alarm on his clock had buzzed, awakening him with a start...

Simply remembering that dream here and now made his body react. Flint shifted uncomfortably in his seat. Better to concentrate on what had come after the dream, after he'd been jarred awake at such an inopportune moment. He had lain there, all sweaty and hot, his bed wrecked, then marshalled his considerable willpower and headed straight to the shower.

Thinking about those miserably icy needles beating down on him at the ungodly hour of 3:30 a.m. alleviated at least a modicum of the sensual pressure. Too bad there wasn't a bucket of cold water handy to pour over himself to totally restore his equilibrium.

"Are those creatures going to stand in the road all day?" Bouvier demanded impatiently. "Can you blast your horn and scare them off, Flint?"

"I can blast the horn, but they won't care." Flint proceeded to do so, and the bison proved him correct by neither budging nor even glancing their way.

"Let's get out and try to herd them." Jack Hall reached for the door handle. "I've had some experience herding sheep and goats."

"Buffalo can't be herded like sheep or goats, or even cattle," said Flint. "In fact, the lack of animals capable of being domesticated in prehistoric North America is one of the reasons why the Indians didn't—"

He paused as Hall jumped out of the van.

"Get back inside immediately or you're cut from the expedition, Hall." Flint's voice rose only slightly, but his tone was hard and cold. "I'll drive you straight to Rapid City and dump you at the airport. That goes for anyone who challenges or ignores my orders as leader of this expedition. This will be my one and only warning to all of you."

To Ashlinn's surprise, Jack Hall, the would-be buffalo herder, climbed back into the van and closed the door.

"I'm back in, mate," muttered Hall. "No need to get bent out of shape."

Ashlinn gazed at Flint. His jaw was set, his dark eyes hooded. He had sounded more matter-of-fact than angry, yet Hall had taken the threat seriously. Or maybe he'd made eye contact with a buffalo and decided against tangling with one.

She was still debating the force of Flint's alpha-male leadership versus the bison's ability to scare when the animals finally moved from the road, leaving it clear for traffic to proceed.

There was a cheer from the men in the back as Flint put the van in gear and they began to move again.

"Would you really do it?" she asked curiously. "Drop someone at the Sioux Falls airport for disobeying you?"

"In a heartbeat, Ashlinn. So if you want to go back to New York early, simply…"

"Try to ride a buffalo? No thanks. The only animal I've ever ridden is an ancient horse at a state fair twenty years ago, which is fine by me. Of course, I really do want to go home. I wish I were back in New York right now," she added, the words tumbling out in a rush.

It suddenly seemed absolutely essential to make sure he remembered that she didn't want to be here. With him. She didn't want to feel at ease with him, didn't want to feel allied with him, and most certainly didn't want to feel this incredible powerful attraction to him.

Practical logistics limited any relationship between them to a brief summer fling. What else could there be? Flint ran Paradise Outdoors based in Sioux Falls and she lived in New York City. What was the point of trying to maintain a long-distance romance? The ending was preordained: the couple either broke up or one made the sacrifice and moved to where the other lived.

That someone would never be Flint, Ashlinn didn't try to kid herself about that. As for herself…

"I love New York," she said emphatically, her face flushing a little. She sounded like a commercial paid for by the city's tourist bureau. But she had a vital point to make. "I'd rather be there than—than any other place on the globe. But I am going to complete this assignment before I leave here."

"Commendable." Flint nodded his approval. "Just hang on for the next two weeks, and then you'll be back in New York for good."

Which is where she belonged, he reminded himself. Where she should have stayed. He wished she had, because she was fast inveigling her way into his mind. He had known her less than twenty-four hours, but he'd already spent too much of that time thinking about her. Wanting her.

Flint swallowed hard. Even worse, he suspected that his intense sexual attraction to her was only part of what drew him to her. Attraction he could dismiss as hormonal, and a contained, controlled person like himself would never be at the mercy of raging hormones. What he couldn't understand, what worried him, was the mysterious bond he felt with her.

Strange…but he could talk to Ashlinn about things he'd never discussed with anyone else. Why? he wondered. What was it about her that induced him to chat instead of ignore her, to confide in her and not shut her out?

He liked her sense of humor, Flint conceded. She seemed to get his too, which gratified him because he'd been told he had no humor in him. More than once.

That rankled. Who wanted to be viewed as a stiff, humorless android? Not Flint, despite his young half sisters' claim that he would rather be killed than crack a smile, which was altogether untrue. Though he could never be mistaken for a stand-up comedian, he knew he possessed a valid sense of humor.

He had never minded being known as "the serious twin," a tag he had been given early on. "The quiet twin" was his other nickname, and his titles persisted to this day. Well, there wasn't a lot of opportunity for joking around while successfully building the family company to a level of success his father had never dreamed of, but that didn't mean he couldn't enjoy a good laugh.

He'd smiled and laughed more since meeting Ashlinn than he had in a long time. The realization caught Flint off-guard. He was self-sufficient and emotionally independent, and while he wasn't a complete loner, he definitely could not be described as "a people person." Truth to tell, there weren't very many people with whom he felt truly comfortable. There were his little sister Eva and a few trusted employees. And of course, most importantly, his twin brother.

Since childhood, he had been content to let Rafe—"the friendly twin, the outgoing one"—take the lead in social situations. Rafe had always been the one to go out and meet people, to establish and maintain friendships; Flint came along when and if he felt like it, assured of a welcome because he was Rafe's twin.

Rafe's career as a lawyer and Flint's as head of Paradise Outdoors hadn't changed the dynamics. The reappearance of the orphaned Camryn and Kaylin, and Rafe's marriage to Holly, had done that.

Now Rafe was all wrapped up in his new family, and the previously tight Paradise triumvirate of Flint, Rafe and Eva no longer prevailed.

Flint glanced over at Ashlinn. She was looking out the window, watching the passing scenery. He wondered what she was thinking; he wanted to engage her attention, to talk to her, laugh with her some more.

Was this how it began with Rafe and Holly? Flint mused. Until he'd met the woman who had quickly become his wife, Rafe had never felt the need for any particular woman, just the need to quench those raging hormones. Flint recalled that Rafe had tried to explain the difference to him, but he hadn't understood. All of a sudden, he was starting to.

The thought struck like a physical blow, and he felt the effects viscerally. Flint took a deep breath and had to remind himself to exhale.

"Have you ever been to New York?" Ashlinn's voice cut through his reverie. She'd turned her head to look at him.

Flint kept his eyes firmly on the road, even though he could feel her soft brown eyes on him. She had the most beautiful, expressive eyes....

"At least once a year, occasionally more often." He sounded brusque. It wasn't easy to talk and gasp for breath at the same time.

"I hate New York," he added fiercely.

He didn't really, but it seemed like a surefire way to create conflict between them. And distance followed conflict, didn't it? He needed that, because his body craved just the opposite, to be as close to her as he could possibly get, in every possible way. Of course, if he were to follow those instincts, complications would surely ensue....

Flint tensed. His priorities were Paradise Outdoors and Eva, he reminded himself sternly. There was no room in his life for complications, or more specifically, Ashlinn Carey. "Yeah, I can't stand the place."

"I figured you probably couldn't," she said.

Her reaction was not what he'd hoped for. Her tone was calm, accepting. She hadn't taken offense, she was neither arguing with him nor freezing him out.

"What's *that* supposed to mean?" he snapped in sheer frustration. "That I'm some ethnic yokel intimidated by big cities? That I prefer buffalo blocking the road to urban gridlock? Well, I'm just as much at home in a four-star restaurant as I am heating canned beans over a campfire."

"Hey now, we'll have none of that, Ashley," said Jack Hall reproachfully. He'd tuned into their conversation just in time to misinterpret it. "There will be no stereotyping by snobby little girls."

"I appreciate your support, Jack," Flint said.

Ashlinn was incensed. Flint made it seem as if she'd actually insulted him when all she had done was attempt to make conversation to pass the time! She almost launched into an impassioned defense, but stopped herself before she said a word.

Why bother trying to explain a few innocuous remarks? If Flint was so eager to take offense, then let him.

Her eyes swept over him, taking in the sharp lines of his profile, his long well-shaped fingers gripping the steering wheel. She averted her gaze before it could drop any lower. She'd been feeling unnerved by their unexpected camaraderie this morning and alarmed by her strong attraction to him. It was certainly safer to be annoyed rather than aroused by him.

Ashlinn stared purposefully out the window at the spectacular terrain surrounding them. Green trees and black hills. Wildflowers and a big, unfamiliar and vaguely creepy bird circling in the sky. She sat up straight. Was it a hawk? A buzzard? She almost forgot her righteous anger and asked Flint.

But she didn't. It could be a directionally challenged seagull, searching for the sea, for all she cared.

Nor did she care a whit about Flint Paradise. Ashlinn gave her hostility free rein. There was nothing special about him. He was a macho clod just like Hall, Yagano, Bouvier and Figueroa. The affinity she'd felt toward him had been a delusion, the result of her over-exhausted imagination. Getting only a couple of hours' sleep tended to have a deleterious effect on a person's mind.

Flint joined in a jocular discussion with the men, something about native dancing or dancers; Ashlinn wasn't sure because she tried not to listen.

She and Flint didn't speak to each other again until he pulled the van into a parking area that he claimed was near their campsite. The intrepid campers were supposed to transport all necessary equipment and supplies to the site to set up camp.

Ashlinn swung her backpack over her shoulders and carried her tent and sleeping bag as she followed the others along a narrow trail through a pine forest that seemed so primordial, she wouldn't have been surprised to see woolly mammoths or saber-toothed tigers running between the trees.

Their campsite was near a swiftly flowing stream. The men were pleased with the location and made plans to fish for their dinner as soon as they assembled their tents. Which they did in record time, noted Ashlinn.

She remained stuck at step three in her attempt to put up her own tent. It was the water-tight component that made it so difficult; if she'd been willing to forgo insolubility, the wretched thing would already be standing.

Finally, she decided to take a break. There was a flat rock atop a small knoll overlooking the stream that was perfect for sitting and watching the water. She saw Koji catch a fish and reject it, tossing it back because it was too small. The other three adventurers were farther upstream, enthusiastically casting their lines.

"Aren't you going to fish?" Flint's voice sounded behind her.

"I don't fish." Ashlinn glanced over her shoulder to see him approaching the rock. "Or hunt," she added, in case he was thinking about offering that as an alternative.

"There are no rules requiring everybody to share their fresh catch on this trip, Ashlinn."

"Survival of the fittest, hmm? Very Darwinian." Her heart began to somersault wildly and she tried her best to ignore it. At least she wasn't hooked up to an electrocardiogram, so there could be no visible evidence of her tumultuous reaction to his presence.

"Nobody is going to starve, but if you don't fish you're going to end up eating something out of a can for dinner every night." Tentatively, Flint walked around the rock and stood beside it. "We have canned stew or hash or spaghetti. Pretty bland fare, but there's plenty of it."

She shrugged. "I saw some hot sauce among the supplies. That'll add tasty zest to anything."

Flint chuckled, in spite of himself. "It's my secret weapon too." He kept his eyes focused straight ahead, watching Bouvier reel in a respectably sized fish. "You haven't put up your tent yet."

"And it's so easy even a twelve-year-old can do it. Yes, I read the Paradise Outdoors spiel in the catalog under the picture. Maybe if I were twelve, I'd have better luck with it."

"As the official guide of this expedition, I was thinking of imposing a strict rule. Nobody does anything until their tents are put up." Flint leaned against the rock.

"Then I'm following orders, sir." Automatically, Ashlinn slid over, making room for him beside her on the rock. "Because I'm not doing anything, am I?"

He sat down, a slight smile quirking the corners of his mouth. "How do I argue with logic like that?"

Their shoulders brushed, their hips touched.

"I'm not looking for an argument," Ashlinn said. Her pulses seemed to be roaring in her ears, almost drowning out the sound of the water rushing over the rocks. "You're the one who was quarrelsome on the drive out here, not me."

"Quarrelsome? What kind of a word is that?" he scoffed.

"I was trying to be tactful. I didn't think it was as insulting as 'hostile.' Or 'belligerent.' Both apply, though."

Flint sucked in his cheeks. "Now who's being 'quarrelsome'?"

"Not me." She reached into the pocket of her jeans and removed an elastic band. "It's too hot to argue," she murmured, gathering her hair in her fist and pulling it up and back into a thick high ponytail. "How can it be so hot in the woods by the water? That campfire tonight is going to feel like an inferno. Maybe I'll have my stew cold, right out of the can."

Flint watched her, like one mesmerized. When she raised her

arms to fix her hair, the pale blue cotton of her T-shirt pulled taut over her breasts, outlining the rounded softness.

"That's better," Ashlinn said, and he assumed she was talking about getting her hair off her neck. She folded her hands and rested them on her lap, like a polite schoolgirl, and resumed watching the fishermen.

Flint stared at the exposed curve of her slender nape. The skin there was milk-white and looked exquisitely soft. He actually had to ball his fingers into fists to keep himself from reaching out and touching.

"It'll be cold at night when the sun goes down and you'll be glad to have the fire." His voice seemed to echo inside his head.

He was excruciatingly aware of the places their bodies were touching. The casual, innocent brushes of their arms. Their shoulders and hips remained in constant proximity because the rock wasn't big enough to accommodate two people without physical contact between them. Flint stretched out his legs in front of him, and his knee bumped hers. She didn't seem to notice, she didn't move away from him. In fact, she didn't move a single muscle at all.

Flint cleared his throat. "But you're right. It's hot today."

"Maybe the rain will cool things down." She glanced up at the sky. "The sky is really getting gray. I wonder when the storm will hit?"

"Rain wasn't predicted when we left Sioux Falls."

"Not for Sioux Falls, it wasn't. But we spent all day driving a million miles in the opposite direction, remember?"

"It wasn't a million miles." Flint fought to suppress a smile, and lost the battle. "It only felt that far. But if you're worried about rain, I have a weather gadget that gauges conditions and makes predictions. It's in my tent."

He stood up and acting instinctively, before his head fully realized what he was about to do, he extended his hand to her. Ashlinn's legs were shorter than his, and she had to step down onto another rock before her feet touched the ground. She placed her hand in his and allowed him to assist her off the rock.

Their fingers interlocked, and for a moment, neither moved. They stood together under the leafy cover of the trees, their hands linked. Flint's gaze dropped to her mouth, and he followed the alluring shape of her lips with his eyes. He couldn't seem to take his eyes off those lips.

"Is a high-tech gadget necessary when a glance at the sky brings the obvious conclusion?" Ashlinn's tone was teasing.

Flint quickly lifted his eyes and met hers. Busted! She'd caught him staring at her.

The uncertainty—or was that anxiety?—on her face belied the light tone of her voice. But he took his cue from her. Ignore the sexual tension between them and keep things flippant. He dropped her hand.

"Clouds can be deceptive. They don't always mean rain." Unable to stop himself, he placed his hand on the small of her back and gently propelled her forward, to the path leading to the campsite a few feet away. "Sometimes a cloudy sky simply means it's a cloudy day."

"Is that a bit of profound wisdom handed down by your forebears?" Ashlinn was pleased she sounded so normal. She definitely wasn't feeling that way.

A pervasive tremor ran through her. She was breathtakingly aware of the warmth of his hand on her back, of his tall strong frame close behind her. All the sounds and sights in the forest seemed to fade into the background; she was totally focused on Flint's presence and her own sensual responses to him. Her heart thundered, sharp arrows of heat pierced her abdomen, streaking lower to her most secret sensitive places.

"If you want to, you can say so in your article." Flint removed his hand from her back to clasp her elbow. He stepped beside her, his grip anchoring her to his side as they walked along the path. "Add a little historical color while you're proclaiming the wonders of Paradise Outdoors and all our products."

"A juxtaposition of old and new. That would work." Ashlinn gamely kept up her end of the conversation, though she felt as if she were on automatic pilot, going through the motions of talking to Flint while a wholly different kind of communication operated, unspoken, between them.

She wondered if he felt it too or maybe she was simply fantasizing, her brain short-circuiting from lack of sleep and the heat and a deluge of pheromones and adrenaline?

They reached the campsite where three tents were loosely circled around the center, which was reserved for the fire. Flint crawled inside his tent, emerging a moment later with a palm-sized device. He pushed a few colored buttons and watched the graphics on the small screen.

"It's official. It's going to rain," he announced.

"Who'd have ever guessed?" Ashlinn arched her brows. She glanced up at the darker clouds that swirled above them. "Thank heavens you brought that thing along."

"Yeah, good thing I did." Flint tried to play it straight but failed. They grinned at each other. "I'd better get your tent up."

He went to the spot she'd selected, where her collapsed tent and other belongings lay. Without even glancing at the instructions, he set to work.

Ashlinn stood and watched. It didn't take long for him to complete the job. "Thanks," she murmured. "I've never been good at assembling things. Courtney and Michelle were the ones to put together our Barbie swimming pool and soda shop."

"I was the one who did that for Eva." Flint smiled at the memory. Kneeling in front of the assembled tent, he reached for her sleeping bag to stash inside it. "I wonder what Eva did with all that stuff?"

"Mom sold our dolls and toys at garage sales over the years." Ashlinn came down on her knees beside him to help shove her things into the tent. "When we see what those things are worth today, we just shriek."

"I saved my entire baseball card and comic book collections. I've been offered plenty for certain ones, but I refuse to sell. I want to keep the collections intact." Flint rose to his feet, extending his hand again to Ashlinn. It was beginning to seem altogether natural for him to assist her.

"You might mention in your article that the president of Paradise Outdoors has personally tested all the merchandise," he suggested. "The company won't stock any products that aren't user-friendly."

"User-friendly to mechanical geniuses, maybe." Ashlinn slipped her hand in his and he pulled her to her feet. "You ought to stock one of those yellow books with the big black print. *Paradise Outdoors for Dummies.*"

They stood facing each other. Flint drew her closer, and Ashlinn went willingly, raising her face to his. His black eyes glimmered with sensual intent. She knew he was going to kiss her, and she wanted him to with every fiber of her being.

"Ashlinn." He spoke her name softly. His hands tightened on her waist as he lowered his head to hers.

Four

Ashlinn's eyelids dropped closed and she waited, barely breathing, for his kiss.

Flint's lips touched hers in a caress so light, so brief, that for a moment she wondered if she had imagined the contact.

She could feel his erection pressing against her, hard and insistent. In marked contrast to that urgency, his hands moved slowly, almost leisurely over her back in long sensuous strokes. Clinging to his shoulders with both hands, Ashlinn shivered with pure pleasure as she savored the solid strength of his chest rubbing against her breasts.

His big hands cupped her bottom, kneading gently as her breathing became rapid and uneven. She felt the tip of his tongue lightly trace the outline of her lips, and they parted, welcoming him inside.

But he did not accept her unspoken invitation. Instead, he lifted his head, making Ashlinn acutely aware of the small space between them. It felt more like a gaping chasm, and she didn't like it. She wanted to be physically connected to him, she wanted him to kiss her.

Her eyes opened and locked with his.

"Flint?" she questioned in a whisper.

"We might be headed places where we shouldn't go," he said huskily. His breath was warm against her mouth.

"And what if we are?" She was surprised by how thick her voice sounded. She didn't want to debate the wisdom or folly of their actions, not now when her lips were tingling and skin was ultra sensitive to his slightest touch.

"You tell me, Ashlinn."

The way he said her name, the way he was looking at her and lazily caressing her sent her spinning in another rapturous rush. "Flint, I want you to…"

"Hey mates! We'd better get the fire started and eat before the rain comes!" Jack Hall's voice boomed through the trees.

Ashlinn gave a small whimper of frustration. Flint muttered something unintelligible and quickly dropped his hands and moved away from her.

"Never saw anything like it. The fish were practically suicidal, just jumping onto our lines." Hall joined them, triumphantly dangling a string of fish. "There'll be plenty for everybody."

"Good job, Jack. I'll get the stove set up and start the fire right away," said Flint, suddenly morphing into the quintessential woodsman. "Need a hand cleaning those fish?"

Ashlinn stood still, unable to move, let alone speak. It was embarrassing to contrast her own dazed condition to Flint's—*he* certainly seemed to have made a complete and speedy recovery.

Was it because she had been lost in passion while he'd remained in control?

Ashlinn was dismayed. It was true. While she had burned for him to kiss her, Flint had retained control of himself, of the situation—and of her, too! She eyed him resentfully. Only seconds ago, she had been melting in his arms, and now he was talking about cleaning fish!

"Grab a knife there, Ash," ordered Jack Hall. "Start chopping. Everybody cooks *and* cleans their own dinner around here, right?"

"I am not going to dissect a fish," Ashlinn stated firmly. "I gagged for a year dissecting creatures in high-school biology lab and vowed I'd never dissect again. So far I haven't, and I don't intend to start now."

"Dissecting in a lab is different from cleaning a freshly caught fish," squawked Hall. "Tell her, Flint."

"Well, for one thing, out here you don't have to identify the fish's internal organs in a quiz." Flint's black eyes gleamed.

"If that's supposed to be a joke, it's not very funny," groused Hall.

"I think it's funny," Ashlinn said quickly. "And anyway, I'm having spaghetti for dinner tonight."

"Spaghetti?" Hall was aghast. "You prefer to eat out of a can when you can have fresh fish?"

"Yes. Is that an offense against the laws of nature?" she retorted.

"I'll clean the fish for her." Flint didn't look up from his fire-starting chores. "Put them down there, Jack, and I'll start on them in a few minutes."

"Oh, Flint, would you clean *my* fish, too?" Koji mocked in a high falsetto. He'd arrived just in time to hear Flint's offer. Rico also joined them, carrying his own catch of the day.

Ashlinn sighed. Being the object of masculine teasing was familiar ground. She'd grown up with brothers who had perfected razzing her to an art form.

"Thank you, Flint, you're very gallant," she said sweetly.

Pretending to be unaware she was being teased had always been a most effective comeback. Her brother Mark would almost gnash his teeth in frustration when she made use of that tactic.

Flint looked up at her. "You're welcome, Ashlinn."

She smiled. So he knew the game, too? She went to sit beside him while he cleaned the fish. Just because she didn't like doing it herself didn't mean she was a faint-hearted sissy who couldn't bear to watch.

Flint cooked her fish and his for dinner, despite additional jests about the leader being the first to break the every-cook-for-himself rule.

"Isn't it preferable to watching her eat spaghetti out of a can, completely ignoring the bounty of nature?" Flint joked back.

"It's certainly preferable to watching her cremate a beautiful fish, if she's as bad a cook as she claims," conceded Bouvier, grimacing.

The group's timing was impeccable. Moments after they'd finished eating, the thunder began. The raindrops began to fall just as they completed their cleanup.

"I guess this is good night, then," said Koji, making a dive for his tent. "See you in the morning at first light."

A bolt of lightning lit the fast-darkening sky, and the wind began to blow.

Ashlinn and Flint stood in front of their tents, which were only a few feet apart. The others were already inside their own tents.

"Remember to zip that inner flap in the front of your tent," Flint said. "It'll keep it watertight."

"I will." Ashlinn nervously ran her fingers along the top of the tent. "I guess we're about to find out if the watertight claim is really true."

"Paradise Outdoors guarantees it," Flint promised, as if nothing more needed to be said.

Maybe it didn't. "Good night, Flint." Ashlinn crawled inside her tent just as the rain escalated from a few heavy drops into a full-fledged torrent.

She sat on the floor of the tent, grateful that it covered the ground, which was going to get very wet. The rain pounded against the tarp so loudly that the claps of thunder were barely audible above it.

Ashlinn looked at her watch. It was just past seven o'clock. Tired as she was, she knew it would be hopeless to try to sleep at this early hour. She'd brought a paperback along, but it was too dark inside the tent to read. Unless she used a flashlight?

She felt around in the darkness for one. Weren't each of the participants supposed to be supplied with a flashlight? She vaguely remembered Flint showing her a flashlight at Paradise Outdoors headquarters this morning, a high-powered model that was guaranteed to "illuminate the darkest night, like the spotlight of a full moon."

Or some such claim. Flint had recited the uses of each product he'd presented to her, but at that predawn hour, Ashlinn's attention span hadn't been up to par.

"Ashlinn, I have your flashlight." Flint's voice sounded outside her tent, above the rain.

She quickly unzipped the flap, and he ducked inside, bringing a gust of cool rainy air in with him. He carried a flashlight that was already switched on. It lit up the interior of the tent.

"I was just looking for it," she exclaimed, astonished by his prescience.

"No, I'm not psychic," Flint immediately dispelled the notion of a preternatural bond between them. "It seemed logical that you would need your flashlight since it's practically pitch black inside these tents at night."

He handed it to her, then ran his palm over his soaked, slicked-down hair. Droplets of water went flying. "Uh, sorry. Didn't mean to bring the rain inside with me."

"It's really coming down hard out there," Ashlinn observed, peeking through the crack provided by the still-open flap. "You don't think the creek will overflow its banks, do you?"

"Do you want to sleep in a life jacket, just in case?"

"Yes. And I'd like to have a canoe and an oar in here, too, just in case." Her droll tone matched his.

They faced each other for a long silent moment, both kneeling on the tent's tarpaulin floor.

"Well, I guess I'd better go," Flint said at last.

"You don't have to run off," she interjected quickly. "I mean, unless you want to." An awkward tension seemed to permeate the tent. "Of course, you're probably busy. You must have a lot of things you need to do."

"Must I?"

Ashlinn writhed inwardly, self-conscious and ill-at-ease, besieged by flashbacks of their near-kiss. Did Flint consider her impulsive invitation a bid to pick up where they left off? *And was it?* she wondered, realizing that she didn't really know herself.

"Thanks for bringing the flashlight." She hoped her face didn't look as hot as it felt. She played with the beam of light, directing it away from herself into the outside through the open crack. "And, um, good night. Again."

"Actually, I have no pressing duties awaiting me in my tent," Flint said dryly.

He zipped the watertight flap and settled himself crosslegged on the floor of the tent.

Ashlinn sat on top of her sleeping bag. She tried to remember the last time she'd felt this way, like a nervous eighthgrader entertaining her big crush at home for the very first time.

Horrors, it had been when she *was* an eighth-grader, on that momentous afternoon when Kevin Gleason had come over after school and they'd sat side-by-side on the sofa in the Carey family living room! It was humiliating to be thrust into the hapless role of anxious adolescent fifteen long years after the fact, but Flint Paradise had that effect on her.

The insight unsettled her.

Rain continued to pound against the tent. The pair sat in silence while Ashlinn played nervously with the flashlight. All she could think of were those moments in Flint's arms, when they'd been about to kiss.

She wondered if he was reliving it too, and decided it would be worse if he was not. It would be too pathetic if she were ruminating over something to which he'd never even given a second thought!

Suddenly, her hand slipped, sending a brilliant beam of light directly into Flint's face.

He reflexively shielded his eyes. "Now I know exactly how a deer caught in the headlights feels. Completely blinded."

"I'm sorry." Ashlinn directed the light away from him. "This is a very bright light," she added, feeling like an idiot.

"Its glow is visible from up to a mile away, which makes it invaluable in an emergency," Flint quoted the company catalog's descriptive blurb. "And don't forget that this flashlight never needs batteries or bulbs. You simply shake it, and that causes a powerful, rare earth magnet to pass through a coil of wire, transforming the motion into electrical energy."

"Amazing," murmured Ashlinn. Flint's enthusiasm for his merchandise was rather endearing. "I think I remember you mentioning that it can also be used underwater," she prompted.

"Yes. And in severe weather too, thanks to the double O-ring seals. You'll be sure to mention all these advantages in your article, won't you? Along with the exact name of the product, so your readers can order them."

"Of course. Everyone will want one. How could they not?" Ashlinn murmured wryly. "Paradise Outdoors is liable to have a worldwide run on these babies."

"Well, that was Carmody's plan, to promote the company and boost sales. With you and the other four writers, we pretty much have the world covered."

It occurred to Ashlinn that if Sam Carmody hadn't ended up in traction, he would've been the one to accompany the group to this park. Somehow, she felt certain that she would not be sitting in edgy proximity with the boyish marketing chief. She'd had quite enough of adult boys; she worked for one.

But there was nothing boyish about Flint. He was mature and responsible. Dependable. And he was *gallant* too, putting up her tent and fixing her dinner. Funny how seductive those practical qualities could be in a man.

Of course, it didn't hurt that Flint was incredibly sexy....

Ashlinn nearly dropped the flashlight.

"If Carmody hadn't been injured, would you have met the members of this expedition?" She knew she was grasping at conversational straws, but it was the best she could do at this disconcerting moment.

"You mean, would I have hosted something along the lines of a wine-and-cheese, get-acquainted reception the night before departure?" Flint laughed. "Believe it or not, Carmody actually suggested it."

"And you said no," Ashlinn guessed.

"Much to Carmody's despair, I don't do receptions. And I saw no reason to get acquainted with the participants in his project." Flint stared at his hands, in a determined effort to keep his eyes off Ashlinn.

He wanted to snatch the flashlight from her because she seemed absolutely fascinated by it and, in turn, indifferent to and unaware of him. It was pretty sad when his competition was a flashlight and he *lost*.

He was hungry for her attention, at least some portion of it. She'd certainly commanded *all* of his attention, Flint mused grimly. He couldn't seem to focus on anything but her.

Though he had intended to spend this evening e-mailing the Paradise Outdoors senior staff members via his laptop's digital hookup, the moment he had switched on his flashlight—the most powerful and reliable model the company sold—he had spied the one issued to Ashlinn, which had mistakenly ended up in his tent.

And that was it for his e-mail and senior staff plans. All he could think about was Ashlinn stuck in total darkness in her tent. He had immediately set out to rectify the situation.

Now here they sat in her brightly lit tent with the rain sounding like marbles being thrown at a tin roof. Making inane small talk when all he wanted to do was to lie her back on that sleeping bag and...

Their eyes met. Flint wondered if the force of his desire was evident in his eyes, because she visibly swallowed and looked...*scared?*

"Do you have a deck of cards?" he asked quickly. Innocuously.

He felt protective toward her; he hated the thought of her

fearing him. But from Ashlinn's point of view, fear was a logical reaction, wasn't it? She was a woman alone in the wilderness with five men she hardly knew. She hardly knew *him*, and he had done nothing to disguise his desire for her.

As Eva often said, "these days, a woman can never be too careful."

Flint knew how he would want his beloved sister treated in a similar situation.

"If you don't, I have some in my tent," he continued. "We could play…" he shrugged. "I don't know, Blackjack? Rummy?"

"Poker? *Not* strip poker," she added succinctly.

"Don't worry, I only play poker for money," he drawled. "So what'll it be? Hearts?"

"How about War? I'll get my cards."

Flint felt oddly elated. She was smiling now, even joking. That had to mean she wasn't afraid of him. It also meant he'd been right to back off.

His elation began to fade a little.

When she retrieved a deck of cards from her backpack and handed it to him, he began to shuffle and deal. "Okay, War it is, but I might need some reminders about the rules. I haven't played that game in years."

"I bet you haven't played *cards* in years," she observed. "Or for that matter, any games at all."

"True. I've always found playing games a boring waste of time. I'd much rather be working."

"So would I. Of course, lately work has been…" She sighed. "Not what it used to be."

"Yes, I believe you mentioned that." He arched his dark brows. "A minute or two after we met."

"Are you expecting me to make another crack about Junior?" Ashlinn grimaced. And then gulped. "I—I guess I have made my feelings about him and his toxic effect on *Tour & Travel* pretty clear, haven't I?"

"Let's just say I know your opinion on your boy boss's

different direction for the magazine. And to call it negative
would be a significant understatement.''

Ashlinn chewed her lower lip thoughtfully. "I guess that was
unprofessional of me, wasn't it?''

Flint made no reply. His eyes were riveted to her mouth,
especially that sensually full lower lip.

No, he told himself. Forget it, he ordered his body that was
already tightening. This is just a friendly card game, and there
won't be anything else. Not for this entire trip.

He was the leader and she was dependent on him, which
made their positions unequal. So wouldn't that make a sexual
affair between them unethical? Like when that rogue senior
resident had hit on Eva when she'd been a first-year med student under his supervision.

The analogy disturbed Flint. He and Rafe had been enraged
on Eva's behalf and begged her to file a complaint against the
guy. Poor little Eva hadn't, though; she'd been too scared.

Scared. The way Ashlinn was scared of him, when he'd
come on too strong? Flint was appalled. He had to let her know
that she was safe with him, as safe as the nonexistent Asher
Carey would've been. He had to treat her like a colleague or
a paying customer, anything but what she actually happened to
be: the one woman he was aching for.

Ashlinn interpreted his long silence as a reproach. She'd said
she had been unprofessional, bad-mouthing her boss and now
Flint had silently agreed. She was mortified.

"Look, pretend I never mentioned Junior and the magazine.
I promise not to say another word about…''

"*Quid pro quo,* Ashlinn. I certainly didn't hold back my
feelings about my half sisters or Carmody's stupid penchant
for taking risks.''

"*Quid pro quo,* huh?'' Ashlinn repeated. He had reduced
their shared confidences and the bond she'd felt developing
between them to that? Something given, an equivalent for
something received.

She glanced down at the cards they had discarded. "I declare
War,'' she said, with startling vehemence.

* * *

During the next two weeks, Ashlinn began to wonder if she had only imagined the sexual electricity that had flared between her and Flint Paradise. Had he really held her, touched her, almost kissed her? Countless times, she turned those crucial moments over in her mind.

No, she *knew* that he would have kissed her if not for Jack Hall's inopportune arrival. She hadn't imagined it, but Flint had obviously forgotten all about it.

Throughout their card games during that rain-soaked first night in camp, she had waited for him to give her some signal, to make a move that indicated he wanted to resume their interrupted kiss. But the evening had remained totally platonic. He had trounced her at War several times, then returned to his tent without looking back at her.

Those charged glances they had exchanged, seemingly from the moment they'd met, also ended that night. During the days and nights that followed, not once did Ashlinn catch Flint stealing a look at her, not once did their eyes meet in a moment of shared understanding or fierce urgency.

The first few days after that near-kiss, Ashlinn felt the incident looming between them. It was like the classic unmentioned-elephant-in-the-parlor metaphor, with a tangible, dominant presence between them, yet neither one alluding to it.

But Flint continued to ignore it, and so she followed his lead and did the same.

He treated her the same way he treated Bouvier, Hall, Yagano, and Figueroa, quick to dispense information about the Paradise Outdoors products and the opportunities available to campers in the park but essentially letting her choose her own activities and proceed at her own pace.

Well, he did clean the extra fish for her and cook her dinner each night, a courtesy he didn't perform for the others.

And he let her carry the Paradise Outdoors electronic mosquito hawk, which allegedly sent mosquitos packing with its imitation sound of a dragonfly, their mortal enemy. She hadn't had a single bite the entire time.

He also set up her tent the three times the group moved to new campsites, to fully sample the park's varying terrains.

And though he'd slowed his pace to lag behind with her when they climbed Harney Peak, Flint didn't try to turn their desultory conversation into anything remotely personal or private. Taking her cue from him, Ashlinn didn't either.

Perhaps it was easy to discount the things Flint had done for her these past two weeks because there were so many things he hadn't done. Despite wanting not to, Ashlinn found herself keeping track.

Flint didn't sit beside her around the campfire or pay another late-night visit to her tent or attempt to be alone with her. He didn't ask her to share a canoe on the lake or explore the caves with him; he didn't single her out to hike or ride their rented mountain bikes with him.

She was part of the group during all activities, but aside from making sure she didn't break her neck, Flint treated her with detached nonchalance.

He didn't touch her, not once.

So Ashlinn pretended she wasn't attracted to Flint. He certainly was uninterested in her now, she was sure of that. His casual friendliness toward her matched that of the other four men.

At least the four international adventurers no longer seemed irritated by her presence. They had become resigned to her diffidence to the outdoors, and at times even seemed to enjoy her company—as much as they could enjoy anyone whose mindset they simply couldn't fathom.

Ashlinn realized that it wasn't solely her sex that set her apart from them. She had also seen them gape incredulously at Flint when he extolled the pleasures and advantage of working in an office. They'd been stunned into silence when he had admitted he didn't mind wearing a suit and tie every day.

The last night of the expedition, as the six sat around the final campfire, Ashlinn exchanged addresses, both e-mail and postal, with the others and promised to include them on her Christmas card list.

"Remember, everyone must let everybody else know when their articles are published—and send copies of the magazines to all," urged Koji.

"Not that we'll be able to read Japanese, Spanish and French," Jack Hall said, turning to Flint and Ashlinn. "The fact that Koji, Rico and Bouvier are all fluent in English makes us look just a tad dumb, doesn't it?"

"Oh, more than a tad," agreed Ashlinn.

"Any idea when the articles will appear?" Flint directed his question to the entire group.

"Eager for Paradise Outdoors to be deluged with orders? That will mean even more time to spend at your office, a thrill for you, Flint." Rico guffawed.

"Yes, a thrill." A serious Flint nodded his affirmative. "Carmody projects a surge of orders for the products mentioned following the publication of each article, and we're prepared to meet the demand."

"What's the word on Carmody, Flint?" asked Koji.

"He'll be out of traction next week and released from the hospital. I expect he'll be back to work then or soon after."

"I shall have to write about Carmody's mistake, believing Ashlinn to be a man named Asher," said Bouvier. "A bit of humor is always welcome in these pieces."

"Glad to serve as the group's laughingstock," Ashlinn replied drolly. "My article is almost finished," she added to nobody in particular. Except she happened to glance at Flint.

And saw him looking at her. A sharp sensation, hot and sweet, shot through her.

"Almost finished?" Hall groaned. "I haven't even started mine yet!"

"She's actually an editor, remember?" Rico pointed out. "Maybe editors write faster than we do."

"Is that true, Ashlinn?" asked Flint.

He was watching her with a steady stare. The flames from the firelight seemed to flicker in his black eyes.

"I don't know." Her mouth was suddenly dry. "Maybe it has to do with the content. This article came easily enough."

She swallowed. "But I sure didn't break any speed records when I wrote my book."

"You wrote a book?" Bouvier was astonished. "What about?"

She grimaced wryly. "Never mind. It wasn't exactly a runaway bestseller."

It had scarcely sold at all! *Hooked!*, a guide to addictive relationships had been at the bottom of the publisher's list; only a scant few bookstores had ordered it and she hadn't even earned out her very modest advance. Ashlinn considered her attempt at authorship to be an embarrassing mistake and made a point of never mentioning her erstwhile book. The fact that she'd blurted out its existence was proof of how truly addled she was by Flint's attentive stare.

"Was it a cookbook? A cookbook by a woman who doesn't cook." Rico laughed at the concept. "No wonder it bombed."

"She wouldn't write a cookbook," Flint said knowingly. "A travel guide, maybe? Of quaint bed-and-breakfast places or something, Ashlinn?"

His eyes lowered to her mouth and Ashlinn felt her lips begin to tingle, as if he were actually touching them.

"Or something," she mumbled.

She wasn't about to confess that she'd written a *relationship* book, especially not to this group. Over nighttime campfires, the four adventurers had made their feelings on relationships clear: they were only interested in short-term, non-binding ones that left them free to pick up and travel at whim. And then there was Flint, deeply involved with his company and needing nothing more.

Even worse, her relationship book was an awful one; the few published reviews of *Hooked!* had been scathing, describing it as "absurd psychobabble" and "junk science with apologies to both junk and science." Ashlinn chalked the entire experience up to a mistake-never-to-be-repeated. Or discussed.

Fortunately, nobody pressed her for any more information about her book. Perhaps they feared she would regale them with mind-numbing descriptions of the quaint little hideaways they believed she'd researched. The subject was dropped, and conversation moved into another area.

Ashlinn stole another quick glance at Flint and saw him gazing intently at her, the way she hadn't seen him look at her the past two weeks, as if he were imprinting her image in his mind. His eyes held hers, trapping her, and she fought a shudder of awareness.

"Our last night here, and all of a sudden it's hot as hell," said Bouvier.

For a horrified moment, Ashlinn thought he had interpreted the unspoken communication between her and Flint, that he'd noticed her skin's heated flush. Then she realized with relief that Bouvier was merely making a bona fide observation about the unusually high temperature for this time of night.

"It's more than the heat, it's the humidity," grumbled Hall. "The kind that makes your clothes stick to your skin. Reminds me of the time I…" He launched into a discourse about some relentlessly humid jungle trek.

The others were quick to share their own tales of miserable climates. Ashlinn listened, feeling a certain fondness for the group. She had grown accustomed to their stories of discomfort and danger—she'd even come to enjoy them in a way. The first thing she intended to buy back in New York was a copy of *The Most Dangerous Places on the Globe*. Thanks to her fellow campers, she already had a working knowledge of most of them.

Listening to their sweltering sagas made her overly aware that her bra was damp and sticking to her skin. A small rivulet of perspiration trickled between her breasts. She picked up her oblong foam-filled, water-resistant seat cushion, the most comfortable and durable of its kind according to the Paradise Outdoors catalog, and moved farther away from the fire.

"Ready to head back to civilization tomorrow?"

Ashlinn turned her head at the sound of Flint's voice. He too had moved, and was now standing alongside her.

Flint sat down beside her, stretching his long legs in front of him. From their first night around the campfire, all five men had roundly rejected the Paradise Outdoors comfy seat cushion, Ashlinn noted. Was it some unspoken cardinal rule that real men sat only on the hard ground? She'd used hers daily to avoid direct contact with that same hard ground.

"It's been pretty civilized out here, thanks to Paradise Outdoors," she replied.

"I hope you'll include that particular endorsement in your article. We'd like to increase our market share of women customers."

"I'll put it in, but I don't know how many women will still be reading *Tour & Travel* after that last gonzo issue Junior insisted on publishing."

Gloom settled over Ashlinn like a cloud, and she acknowledged to herself that it had little to do with the magazine's transformation. This was her last night in South Dakota, her last night in the spectacular Black Hills—and her last night with Flint.

Though he was seated next to her, he wasn't particularly close, remaining at least an arm's length away. He had avoided sitting near her since their first night in camp, always placing himself between two of the men.

And now, it was their last night here. After he drove her to the Sioux Falls airport tomorrow, she would never see Flint Paradise again.

A sense of loss filled her, and Ashlinn immediately tried to talk herself out of it. Instead of mourning what hadn't happened, she should be celebrating her own judgment and control. Rather than indulging in a hot fling with Flint, she had made a mature decision not to lose her head over a fleeting summer romance, and she'd stuck to it.

Never mind that except for the first day, Flint hadn't given her an iota of encouragement, taunted a derisive inner voice, the one that always made her face the truth even when she didn't particularly want to, because it hurt too much.

What if she had encouraged Flint? Ashlinn wondered, an odd restlessness churning within her. What if she'd tried to break through his wall of reserve and end the polite distance between them?

You mean, what if you'd thrown yourself at Flint? countered her mature, controlled superego, striving to squash that renegade uprising of regret. *What if you'd made a total fool of yourself by chasing a man who made it clear he wasn't interested in you? How would you be feeling right now, if you'd done that?*

Yes, she should definitely be congratulating herself on maintaining her pride and not succumbing to impulse. Or to need or desire.

Ashlinn sighed. At this rate, she was going to propel herself into a full-blown depression.

"Bored?" asked Flint. "I guess you've heard one too many adventure stories from the old gang, huh?"

He had mistaken her melancholy sigh for one of boredom. Ashlinn wasn't about to correct him. "Pretty much, I guess," she murmured vaguely.

"Feel like taking a swim?"

Her jaw dropped. "Swim? Now?"

"Sure. It's hot enough."

Flint's fingers went to the top of his blue poplin shirt—heralded in the Paradise Outdoors catalog for its tight cotton weave that repelled rain, thorns and insects yet allowed the wearer's skin to breathe—and he began to unfasten the buttons. "Look at the water. Doesn't it look inviting?"

His gaze was fixed on the mountain lake beyond the trees, some thirty yards from their campsite. Ashlinn's eyes remained riveted on his shirt, which was now opened to where it was tucked into the waistband of his jeans.

Flint stood up, pulled his shirt from beneath his belt and continued unbuttoning. "It'll be refreshing."

"Said the serpent as he offered Eve a bite of the apple," muttered Ashlinn under her breath.

Flint held out his hand to her. "Come on."

It seemed that mature, controlled Ashlinn hadn't managed to quash those restless stirrings, after all. They resurfaced now, stronger and more compelling than ever. Virtually impossible to resist.

"It is hot out tonight, and the tent will probably feel like a furnace," she reasoned aloud. "Why hurry to get inside it?"

"My thoughts exactly." Flint flexed his fingers, his arm still outstretched to her.

Ashlinn put her hand in his, and he pulled her to her feet. They faced each other, their hands linked.

The group around the campfire was breaking up. Hall doused the flames and everybody retired to their tents, calling their good-nights.

Ashlinn and Flint stood in silence. Neither mentioned the late-night swim or invited the others to join them.

"I—I'll just put on my bathing suit," Ashlinn heard herself say. "I'll be ready in a minute."

Her voice sounded faraway, as if it had taken leave of her and now belonged to someone else. Maybe the same thing had happened to her judgment and self-control? That would certainly explain a lot.

"No skinny-dipping for you?" The corners of Flint's lips quirked into a slight smile.

"Or for you," she said firmly.

No, her judgment and self-control were still with her, Ashlinn assured herself. She was simply going to enjoy a refreshing swim in the lake on this last night of her assignment. And because it was unsafe to swim alone—Water Safety Rule Number One—Flint was accompanying her. That's all there was to it.

She crawled into her tent and pulled a bathing suit from a pocket of her backpack. It was a quick-to-dry Paradise Outdoors number that performed as promised but was rather lacking in the style department. A modestly cut, mud-brown knit maillot, the suit was fairly devoid of sex appeal, intended for serious swimming, not lolling on a beach attracting admiring glances.

Just what she needed for tonight. She wanted to swim, not to be admired by Flint, Ashlinn insisted to herself as she pulled a loose cotton T-shirt and boxers—her usual camp sleeping attire—over her suit. She left on her socks and sneakers, not wanting to risk stubbing her toes on a rock or root or stepping on some ominous woodland creature on the walk to the water's edge.

Her pulse was racing as she stepped outside the tent. She felt excited and anxious, burning with energy and a dizzying anticipation.

She reminded herself once more that she was merely going for a swim with a campmate, who hadn't even been upgraded to the status of friend.

"Ready?" Flint was waiting for her, his premier flashlight in hand.

Ashlinn nodded and followed him along the narrow path to the lake. The sky was bright with starlight, although the crescent moon provided only an additional sliver of illumination.

The lights from the night sky shone on the smooth expanse of Flint's back, and Ashlinn watched as shadows played across it. His skin was bare; he wore only a pair of loose jeans and moccasins. Her eyes traveled over him, from his sleek black hair, over the glowing bronze of his back and his long denim-clad legs.

She knew she had to keep moving. If she were to stop and think…

But she didn't. As soon as they reached the water's edge, without pausing to glance at Flint again, Ashlinn yanked off her clothes and shoes, arranging them neatly on the rocky shore safely away from the lapping of the waves.

"I'll stand the flashlight on its base and leave it on," Flint said. "It'll serve as a beacon for us here on the shore."

Ashlinn made no reply. Nor did she wait for Flint to peel off his jeans and join her in testing the waters. Keeping her eyes focused straight ahead, she waded into the lake.

The water was cool and felt wonderful against her hot flushed skin. Ashlinn kept walking until the water almost reached her shoulders.

Tentatively, she bent forward and touched her face to the

water. She felt the refreshing chill on her forehead, on her cheeks.

And then a hand clasped her neck. She gasped and jerked herself upright.

"I didn't hear you! You sneaked up on me!"

"An old trick, passed down through the generations." Flint chuckled. He was standing behind her, his fingers wrapped around her nape. The water barely reached his waist.

"Don't you dare try to dunk me!" warned Ashlinn. Her breathing was erratic, coming in short spurts and her voice lacked the firmness required for her command.

"Don't want to get your hair wet?" he mocked. With his other hand, he gave her ponytail a light tug.

"And if I said I didn't, you would push my head under so fast…"

"Not me! Bouvier might do something like that, maybe Koji and Rico, too. Hall definitely would." Flint's thumb began to rub the nape of her neck. "But I'm a gentleman, Ashlinn."

Desire pooled sharp and deep in her belly. Her nipples were tight and hard as they pressed against the knit material of her suit.

"Are you?" she whispered.

Five

"**Y**ou mean you haven't noticed? I've been on my best be-havior these past two weeks. A *perfect* gentleman." Flint's voice was tinged with irony.

He dropped his hand from her neck and began to walk far-ther into the lake.

"You've been the ideal expedition guide," Ashlinn called to him. "An exemplary, irreproachable host representing Par-adise Outdoors."

Flint didn't look back.

Ashlinn remained where she was, watching the water level rise higher on his body as he went in deeper. It reached his chest, then his shoulders, but he kept on moving. She debated whether to follow, realizing that because of the differences in their heights, the water out there would be over her head while he was still on his feet.

A kind of figurative description of what had already hap-pened between them, Ashlinn decided; she was in way over her head with Flint Paradise while he'd kept his feet firmly on

the ground in regard to her. His fraternal behavior toward her
these past two weeks unmistakably confirmed it.

But it was hard to stay tense or uncertain in the warm dark
water, with the velvety sky overhead sparkling with a zillion
tiny lights. Ashlinn gave in to the soothing lull of the water
and put all thoughts on hold.

She flipped over to her back and arched, tilting her head
back. She loved to float, and the calm lake water was perfect
for it. The air was warm on her exposed skin, while the water
cooled the back of her, creating an exquisitely sensuous contrast.

Ashlinn stretched her arms over her head, pointed her toes
and floated blissfully. After a while, she began to paddle lightly
with her arms and kick her legs in swift scissors motion.

Suddenly, something grabbed her foot and pulled. Startled,
Ashlinn went underwater, resurfacing a moment later. She
coughed and gulped for air as she felt for the bottom with her
toes.

And didn't find it.

Her floating and backstroking must have carried her out
much farther than she'd realized, well beyond where she could
stand.

And then she felt hands grasp her under her arms, holding
her up, keeping her head out of the water. Finally catching her
breath, Ashlinn opened her eyes to see Flint. He was treading
water while keeping a firm grip on her.

"Sorry." His hair was wet and slicked back. "I wasn't trying to drown you." He smiled ruefully. "You said not to dunk
you, but I couldn't resist."

Ashlinn recalled her past as a bossy kid officiously issuing
commands that others found impossible not to defy. It seemed
she still possessed that old knack.

"I'm all right." She tried to wriggle out of his hold and
coughed again.

"Relax. Catch your breath." Flint didn't let her go. "Hope
I didn't blow my reputation as exemplary, irreproachable host

and ideal guide." His inflection and tone made the words sound downright insulting.

"I meant that as a compliment, you know," said Ashlinn, still breathless. But she suspected it wasn't so much from a lack of oxygen anymore.

Flint's big hands served as anchors to keep her just inches away from him while they both continued to tread water with their legs. Several times, their lower limbs brushed and nearly became entangled.

Ashlinn felt sparks along each point of contact between them. She gave up trying to escape and fastened her hands on his forearms, to better steady herself.

Experimenting a little, she stopped treading and kept her legs still. Nothing happened. She didn't go under; Flint was keeping them both afloat.

"Yeah, well, you know what they say about exemplary, irreproachable hosts and ideal guides." Flint began to propel himself backwards, kicking his powerful legs while taking care to keep their heads above water as he towed her along.

"What do they say?" quizzed Ashlinn.

"That exemplary, irreproachable hosts and ideal guides finish last."

"They—I never heard anyone say that," she countered.

"You never heard the old platitude 'nice guys finish last'? Come on, Ashlinn, everybody's heard that one."

"Well, sure, but..."

"Exemplary, irreproachable hosts, ideal guides and nice guys are interchangeable. Fungible. Six of one, half dozen of another."

"Oh." She thought about that for a moment while gliding through the water. "I'm not sure what you're getting at, Flint."

"Don't have the slightest idea, huh?" His gaze was hot and sharp. "I really have been the perfect gentleman."

Her blood surged wildly in response to that intent black stare of his. After enduring two weeks of him treating her like she was one of the guys, having him look at her in that particular way was exhilarating. Intoxicating.

"There's a sandbar out here somewhere," he said, continuing to tow her along. "I think we're almost there."

A short while later, he stopped and felt for the ground with his feet. "We're on the bar now. I can stand."

"I don't think I can."

Since the water level reached Flint's shoulders, Ashlinn *knew* she couldn't stand, but she tried anyway, stretching out her legs and reaching for the sandy bottom with her toes. The waters closed over her head.

A millisecond later, Flint hauled her up, pulling her to him.

"No, I can't touch ground." She felt the need to state the obvious. Their faces were close, so close. Ashlinn shivered.

"Cold?" Flint was immediately solicitous.

"No." She shook her head. "No, I'm just…" Words failed her. She could hardly tell him she was ablaze with a feverish urgency, the force of which she'd never known. But it was certainly safe to say, "I'm not cold."

Perhaps Flint interpreted the tremor in her voice, in her body, to that of anxiety, from being far out in the lake on a dark night. Perhaps.

"Don't worry, I'll keep you from going under." His voice was silky smooth, flowing over her like the supple lake waters.

Ashlinn turned her head a little to look back at the shore. They were at least several hundred yards from land, well into the middle of the lake.

"I can see your flashlight shining on the beach," she murmured. "It's so bright it can probably be seen from outer space. Maybe it'll signal a passing UFO."

"Don't ever mention that thought to Carmody. He would want to incorporate it in the catalog description, and we already verge mighty close on hyperbole as it is."

"You think?" Her dark eyes danced. "I didn't realize you'd noticed. I mean, you talk the Paradise Outdoors talk so well."

"Don't I, though? But I noticed, Ashlinn. I notice everything."

The way he said it, the way he was looking at her, made Ashlinn wonder if he was still talking about the Paradise Outdoors catalog. Made her suspect that he was not. She ran the tip of her tongue over her top lip, not because it was dry. Because she was nervous.

But it wasn't nervous anxiety pumping through her veins; it was a heady, thrilling, delicious kind of nervousness that the ever-cool, self-contained Ashlinn Carey had never experienced. Until now.

She opened her mouth to speak, then realized she could think of nothing to say. She couldn't think at all.

Flint's eyes focused on her parted lips. ''Just put your hands on my shoulders and rest for a little while, Ashlinn. I'll hold you.''

Slowly, hesitantly, she laid her hands on his shoulders, feeling the water-slicked muscles ripple beneath her palms. The action brought her body fully against his. They were now belly-to-belly, and Flint clamped his hands around her waist.

Ashlinn made a most shocking discovery. ''You're not wearing a bathing suit!''

''I'm not?'' Flint laughed, feigning surprise.

Every inch of her skin, even the parts covered by her bathing suit—*especially those parts*—felt as if they were burning with a heat unquenchable by the cool water. She was on fire, sensual fire.

''Flint!'' she admonished severely.

However, her conduct was at odds with her scolding tone. She didn't move away from him, she kept her hands firmly clasped around his shoulders. And the expression on her face was intense and yearning as her eyes held his.

Flint tightened his fingers around her waist and arched her even closer, and more provocatively, to him. ''Putting on a suit at this hour of the night when nobody but you and I are in the lake seemed like a monumental waste of time, Ashlinn.''

''Oh, did it?''

She felt his legs against hers. Even in the water, she was enticingly aware of the masculine contrast—the wiry hair covering his skin, the powerful muscles—to her own limbs. Hers were smooth; she'd faithfully shaved her legs for the duration of the trip, even as she had silently mocked herself for doing so. Now she was glad because her skin, from thigh to ankle, was smooth to the touch.

"Yeah. And think of my noble Sioux ancestors, hundreds of years ago, camping around this lake on a hot summer night." Flint's hands moved slowly over her hips. "Can you imagine one of them wearing a bathing suit in the water? The poor soul would've been laughed out of the tribe."

She imagined the scene. "That's true—for back then. But…"

"I know, I know. That was then, this is now." He released her at once and swam a few feet away from her in a widening circle.

Ashlinn began treading water to keep afloat and admitted to herself that this was not what she'd had in mind.

"I haven't rested long enough to swim back to shore." She sucked in her fiery cheeks. How could she blush so in cool water? It seemed physiologically impossible, yet she just knew her entire body was bright crimson.

Flint swam back to her. "Do you need some help?"

"Yes." She reached out for him, relinquishing herself to his arms, his strength.

Neither said anything. When it became obvious that Flint wasn't going to break the silence, Ashlinn felt compelled to supply a conversational gambit. "I wonder if women back in primitive times had the same freedom as men? Would they have to wear some type of clothing when they went in the water?"

"Who knows? Would it be too harsh to add, who cares? I mean, a walk down costume history lane doesn't interest me, especially not now." Flint slipped his thigh between hers.

Ashlinn drew a sharp breath.

"No?" He looked down at her, his eyes as dark and deep as the waters of the lake. "Am I reading you wrong, Ashlinn? Do you want to go back to shore now?"

She wondered how he could think so, how he could possibly ask such a question when her behavior made the answer so obvious. Yet the very fact that he hadn't assumed her compliance was reassuring. And so very Flint-like. After spending two weeks with him she knew she was safe with him—if she wanted to be.

"I like it out here," Ashlinn whispered, feeling both shy and bold, a paradoxical response she couldn't begin to analyze. Not that she had any inclination to do any analyzing, not now, not here. She wanted to act, to feel…

His lips grazed her temple. "So do I."

Their eyes clung. Ashlinn's fingertips seemed to be moving of their own volition, following the line of his collarbone to the hard cord of his neck. She felt the heavy thud of his pulse there and then raised her hand to the curve of his jaw.

"I never act on impulse." Flint turned his head slightly so that his cheek was resting against her palm. "Well, almost never."

"Neither do I." Her thumb wandered to his mouth and lightly caressed his lower lip. "I have an endless capacity to overthink everything. But I… I'm sick of doing that…especially right now."

"Glad to hear it." He gave a short, rough laugh. "Because I'm about to act on impulse right now."

Letting out a soft groan, he crushed her to him, his mouth opening over hers, his tongue penetrating the moist warmth of her mouth.

Ashlinn clung to him, her tongue meeting his stroke for stroke. This was what she'd been wanting, what she'd dreamed of while lying in her sleeping bag in the tent, night after night.

Their kiss was deep and slow and wet, an intimate and tender mating that grew progressively wilder and harder and hotter.

His hands molded her to him and she felt his erection, hard and insistent, throbbing against her. Her body seemed to be melting like an ice cube in the rippling water. Softening. Liquefying.

Recklessly, she returned his caresses, her palms gliding over him, his shoulders, his back, feeling the strong muscles flex. Feeling daring and bold, she lowered her hands to his buttocks that were bare and muscular, the skin smooth and cool. Desire crested and surged fiercely within her.

Want me, she whispered to him in her head. *Want me, Flint...*

"I do." His lips were against her ear, and she felt the words as she heard them.

It was only then that Ashlinn realized she had spoken her heartfelt longing aloud. She couldn't believe that she had actually voiced her need to him. Pleaded with him. It was so out of character for her. Had she sounded desperate? Her often-repeated words of advice, given so freely to Courtney and Michelle and numerous friends, rang in her ears, mocking her: "Desperation is never attractive."

Until this moment, Ashlinn had never felt desperate. Now, she finally comprehended what desperation was all about.

"I've wanted you every minute of this entire trip," Flint said huskily. "You know that, Ashlinn."

She was unnerved by how very badly she wanted his words to be true. A cruel pang of doubt assailed her. Did Flint mean it, or had he merely said that because she'd said it first, and he wasn't unwilling to participate in an impromptu, late-night tryst?

"No, I didn't know." Ashlinn drew back a little, alarmed and embarrassed. Aroused and on fire. How did Flint evoke such a range of emotions in her? And sometimes, all at the same time!

"Ashlinn, how could you not?" Flint nipped at her lips. Rubbed them with his own.

She was still a little wary, but more than willing to be convinced by him. "But how could I when you never gave me a clue?"

"Never gave you a clue?" he echoed, incredulous. "It was embarrassingly obvious about how I felt. You heard the other guys constantly kidding me about how I did everything for you, and..."

"They needled you because you took your guide duties so seriously," Ashlinn interrupted. "They considered you overly conscientious and me an inept drag. They were delighted that it was you who was stuck dealing with my lack of skills, not them. *That's* why they were always kidding you, Flint.''

"Baby, have you got it wrong!" he growled. "The guys found it hilarious that I gazed at you like a lovesick schoolboy while you never even looked my way."

"You didn't gaze at me at all!" Ashlinn blurted out. "I know that for a fact because I did look your way, lots of times. Too many times. And you weren't ever looking back."

"Ashlinn, I watched you constantly. I wanted to take care of you, I wanted to do things for you—and not because I'm such an exemplary guide and host, either. You didn't see me waiting on the guys hand and foot, did you?"

"You didn't wait on me hand and foot during this trip."

"Of course I did! I wanted to show you that I, how I... But I didn't want to scare you—" He broke off, shaking his head. "Look, it's no use arguing."

"I agree, it's incredibly stupid," Ashlinn cut in again. "We're arguing about wanting each other."

"I don't have an argument for that, Ashlinn."

His hand cupped her breast, and she whimpered. His fingers traced the outline of her nipple, so taut and prominent against the knit material of her swimsuit.

"I've wanted you since the night we met at the airport," he confessed hoarsely. His lips played with hers between words as he continued to fondle her breast. "That first day in camp when I was holding you, and then Hall showed up with those damn fish..." He made a sound that was a combination laugh and groan.

"You went from almost kissing me to cleaning and cooking those fish without missing a beat." She sounded a trifle whiny, Ashlinn conceded. She hoped he hadn't noticed and made concerted effort to sound matter-of-fact. "When you didn't try to kiss me again that night in the tent—or even to come near me during the entire trip—I figured you weren't interested."

The suggestion of a smile tilted his lips. "And you wanted me to be interested, Ashlinn?" His voice was deep and low.

"Oh, why bother to deny it?" Ashlinn was exasperated, with herself, with him. His hand on her breast, his gentle arousing fingers, seemed to have caused a meltdown of all her defenses. She couldn't play it cool, even if she wanted to. "Yes!"

Flint actually laughed. "You sound downright peeved."

"Are you going to assume I'm angry and swim away?" she challenged.

"And then you would assume I'm not interested in you, wouldn't you? When nothing could be further from the truth." Carefully, he slipped the straps of her swimsuit over her shoulders. "Seems like we've had spectacular success in misinterpreting each other, haven't we?"

"It sounds as if we've been at cross purposes for the past two weeks." Ashlinn sighed. "You looking at me, me looking at you, and somehow neither of us seeing anything."

"That first night in the tent when I didn't kiss you..." Flint slid his hands along her arms, taking the straps of her suit down to her wrists. "I wanted to, Ashlinn. Badly. But you looked scared and the last thing I wanted to do was to frighten you."

"The only thing that scared me that night was the thought of you not kissing me. I wanted you to so much. And you didn't." Her voice was raw. "I've never been afraid of you, Flint."

She thought of the two weeks of frustration they'd both endured. It seemed so stupid. Why had they waited until tonight to confront each other?

"Just to avoid any more possible misinterpretations..." Flint lowered the bodice of her suit to her waist, baring her breasts to him. His hands cupped the rounded softness and her warm flesh filled his hands. "Are you letting me do this because you want it too, or because you think you have to because I'm the leader of the group?"

"We've spent every day for the past two weeks together, Flint. Do I strike you as the groupie type?" She looked up at him from under her lashes, her gaze sultry. "Or the type of insipid twit who would give in to a man because I thought I *had* to?"

"Definitely not." He nipped at her neck. "You're anything but an insipid twit, Ashlinn."

"Thank you. You say the sweetest things."

Flint grinned, his teeth gleaming white amid the shadows on his face. "You have this knack of making me want to laugh right in the middle of ravishing you." His fingers teased her swollen nipples. "I just want to hear you say you want me, too. Right here, right now."

Ashlinn moaned softly. His hands felt so good. She wanted this, she wanted him.

"Yes." If he demanded her complete acquiescence, her total surrender, she would give it to him. "I want you, Flint. Right here, right now."

Gazes locked, he lifted her higher, and she wrapped her legs around his waist.

Flint dipped his head, touching his lips to her breasts. His tongue laved first one, then the other sensitive peak, bathing them in moist heat, providing yet another sensuous contrast to the cool water, the warm dry air.

Need roared through her like wildfire. She cradled his head, threading her fingers through his dark sleek hair. When he drew one tight bud into his mouth and suckled rhythmically, Ashlinn arched against him with a hungry little cry.

"Let's get you out of that suit," Flint said huskily, tugging at it.

Ashlinn eagerly assisted. She'd never felt like this before, almost delirious with urgency, her loins clenching, aching with need. Liquid heat pooled between her legs as a pleasure so intense it bordered on pain radiated through her.

Her bathing suit was gone, and she felt the long length of his nude body against hers. The sensation was fantastic, her breasts nestled against the hard wall of his chest, the sensitive tips tingling, his sex pressing hot and throbbing against her swollen softness.

"How did we reach this stage so quickly?" she murmured dizzily.

"Quickly?" He laughed softly. "It feels more like an eternity of waiting to me, Ashlinn."

"For me, too," she heard herself agreeing, and decided it was another one of those Flint-inspired paradoxes. Setting a speed record for arousal, reaching the need for consummation with astonishing haste, yet seemingly waiting forever for it.

Ashlinn closed her eyes as she wrapped herself around him, opening herself to him. He accepted the enticing feminine invitation immediately, cupping her bottom, positioning her to receive him.

He thrust inside her. She gasped at his size and strength. It had been a long time for her, and her body was unaccustomed to this masculine invasion.

She felt stretched and burning hot inside and for a few seconds, overmatched and overwhelmed. But an instant later, her inner muscles contracted and flexed, commencing the sensuous process of adjusting her body to his.

Oh yes, this was much better. Ashlinn dug her fingers into his back, hard.

"Too much?" Flint was panting now. "Should I stop?"

"Don't even think of it," she said with such ferocity that he immediately obliged with another stroke, taking him even deeper inside her, filling her completely.

For a moment, it was enough and they remained that way, their bodies merged, holding each other in a dreamy state of blissful fusion.

And then her hips began to move, slowly at first, then faster, pacing to the rhythm of his thrusts. The tempo increased in a frenzy of mutual abandon. Control vanished as both were caught up in the wild pleasures of sheer physical ecstasy.

Her neck arched, her head back, Ashlinn clung to him as passion built and spun and soared within her. She tried to control the urgency of immediate need by savoring the exquisite pleasures of postponement, but soon, very soon, she felt the sweet heat of release begin to unfurl within her.

She gave up and gave in to it, crying his name as the intensity shattered into shimmering waves that engulfed her entire body. With a low guttural moan, Flint rocked against her one last time, burying himself deep inside her and spilling his seed.

They remained that way, still joined together, Flint standing on the sandbar in the water holding Ashlinn. She languidly caressed her way over his shoulders, his neck, across the hard muscles of his back. She found no need for words; their silence was serene and deeply companionable.

They shared a lingering, sweetly tender kiss....

An undeterminable length of time later, the wind began to pick up, blowing across the lake, growing cooler as it did. Without the warming breeze, the temperature of the water started to feel chilly.

Ashlinn shivered, and this time Flint didn't ask if she was cold, he knew because his skin was covered with the same goose bumps as hers.

"We should get back now," he said, rubbing his hands up and down her arms to warm her. "It would be foolish to risk hypothermia out here."

"Too bad Paradise Outdoors doesn't carry wet suits. They'd be useful for times like these." Ashlinn's teeth began to chatter.

"Our catalog carries the most superior wet suits available in the world today," Flint replied. "But we—Carmody and I—didn't consider it necessary to supply them to members of the expedition."

Ashlinn drew back a little. "You sound like Robo-Executive, citing catalog items, all with claims of superior quality, of course. Next you'll be quoting projected sales figures and the pros and cons of taking a private company public."

What was startling—and disturbing—was that he sounded nothing at all like the passionate man who had just become her lover, she added silently, unable to voice that thought aloud.

"Sorry to bore you." This time it was his turn to pull back, not very much, but enough for his withdrawal from within her.

"I didn't say that." She felt empty and hollow without him.

It was disconcerting to realize how much she wanted him inside her again. Ashlinn tensed. "Must you be so flippant?"

"What do you call your Robo-Executive remark? If that's not flippant, I don't know what is."

"So you're just following my lead? Responding in kind?" Her voice was laced with disbelief. *He'd* been the first to turn detached and then glib. Not her. It was so obvious that she was merely responding in kind to him.

"Yes," affirmed Flint.

Ashlinn stared at him, wishing for more light. The thin beam from the crescent moon had been perfect for their impetuous lovemaking in the water, but at this moment, she could really use the world-class Paradise Outdoors flashlight to shine on his face so she might divine a clue as to what was visible there. She hoped it wasn't what she was divining from his tone and his words.

Suddenly, their post-coital silence struck her as problematic instead of sweet. Because silence enabled one to misinterpret, to fill the void with the wrong messages. Had she been wrong believing that he'd shared her feelings of connectedness between them? That he had experienced the same profound bonding she had?

If she'd been wrong about that, then she was correct now. And right now, she was beginning to suspect that having satisfied his lust, he found her tiresome.

Anxiety seized her, forceful and intense. She and Flint already had a track record of misinterpreting each other for the past two weeks. But they had discussed all that, they'd put it behind them and moved on to a new level in their relationship. Hadn't they?

Ashlinn's heart seemed to plunge at the same moment her stomach lurched, meeting somewhere in her middle. The sensation was strange, not to mention sickening. She wanted to talk to Flint; they *needed* to talk as much as earlier they'd needed to make love.

It was the only way to prevent a rift based on misunderstanding. She felt them headed that way. "Flint, I..."

"We'll swim back, spotting for each other," he ordered in brisk scout leader tones. "Come on, let's get started. If you feel tired and want to pause to rest, let me know."

After being content to let time stand still, he was certainly in a rush to get back to shore. Ashlinn's apprehension accelerated frantically. She could *feel* Flint's impatience. It was almost palpable.

If she hadn't unwrapped her arms and legs from around him, she guessed he would've done it himself. And she couldn't help herself from wondering if his haste to untangle himself from her physically might well be inspired by his desire to emotionally disengage from her.

It was a heart-stopping thought, immediately followed by another one.

"My bathing suit!" Ashlinn exclaimed, suddenly, excruciatingly aware that she was naked.

It hadn't mattered before, when she believed she and Flint were so in tune. So in love!

Ashlinn's face burned. *In love?* Where had that come from? It was something her romantic, rose-colored-glasses-wearing stepsister Michelle might think. Her sister Courtney too. *A couple caught up in the throes of passion made love because they were in love?* Yes, believing that was pure Courtney and so very Michelle.

It certainly wasn't the way her own mind worked, Ashlinn reminded herself. She was the realist who was able to view sex and love as the separate entities they were, she was the cool sophisticate whom her sisters and brothers had dubbed cynical.

"You don't need your suit, Ashlinn. It's just the two of us out here."

Ashlinn flinched. He sounded edgy at best, aggravated at worst. The way Bouvier had sounded when she'd dropped her paddle into the lake while canoeing. Flint had seen what happened from his own canoe, dove into the water and retrieved it for her without censure.

Well, as he'd phrased it himself earlier, "That was then, this was now."

"I need my suit!" Her voice was high and panicky now. She flailed her arms around in the water, feeling for her suit. "I can't walk back to the tent with nothing on. What if the other guys are up and out of their tents? No, I won't do it."

"You've picked a fine time to suddenly turn modest as a— a pilgrim or something." There was an unmistakable scowl in Flint's voice.

"I haven't suddenly *turned* modest! In case you didn't notice, I didn't go around flaunting myself on this trip. I *am* modest." She began to swim to the left, then to the right, alternately stretching her limbs in hopes of hooking the suit.

"We left clothes on the shore, remember? You won't have to walk naked through the woods."

Now Flint sounded like Jack Hall glibly mocking her. Ashlinn's temper flared anew. She didn't knuckle under to taunts; she never had, and she wasn't about to start now. Any thoughts of abandoning her search were instantly forgotten.

"I want that suit. I'll find it if it means staying out here till daylight. Oh, where is it?" she exclaimed, frustration increasing at every failed attempt. "It's supposed to float. Isn't that one of the many claims the stupid catalog makes about it to justify the pricey cost?"

She knew it was the wrong thing to say the moment she uttered the words. If there was anything absolutely guaranteed to infuriate Flint Paradise, it was attacking his company. Better she had called *him* stupid and spared the catalog!

"Our catalog is not stupid," Flint replied in tones as frozen as an iceberg. Maybe even colder. "Furthermore, our prices are very fair. Paradise Outdoors is proud of never gouging our customers. We offer quality merchandise, and those who demand the best are willing to pay for it."

Maybe she should apologize for the insults? Name-calling was a favorite tactic of Junior's, juvenile and...well, stupid.

Ashlinn was considering what to say when Flint called out, "I've got it. Floating, just as guaranteed. Here." He tossed it to her.

His was not a tone of voice that evoked apologies. She snatched the suit and said nothing.

"Put it on when we get to the shore. Now let's go, Ashlinn."

She thought of the flashlight, shining brighter than a lighthouse on the rocky beach. The prospect of emerging naked from the lake, of walking through the shallow waters to fetch her clothes on shore, while literally spotlighted, was paralyzing. Flint would be watching her—or else he wouldn't because he couldn't be bothered to look. She couldn't face either alternative.

"I'm putting the suit on right now," Ashlinn announced. "Consider it the act of a—a modest pilgrim."

"You're wasting time. For crying out loud, Ashlinn, your teeth are chattering, your lips are blue and you're…"

"I'm fine!" she snapped, struggling into the suit. It wasn't easy to do while treading water in the dark, but her anger fueled her, all but banishing the symptoms of the cold. "You're projecting your own discomfort onto me. If you're cold, feel free to start swimming back. I don't need you to wait around for me."

"I said I would wait." He spoke through clenched teeth. "And I will."

Flint continued to swim around her, and Ashlinn resisted the urge to tell him to look away. She didn't want him observing her thrashing about as she dressed, but far worse was the prospect of hearing him make some glib reply. If he were to toss off a careless, "You've got nothing I haven't seen before," or something similar, she knew she would be crushed.

But Flint said nothing, and the moment her suit was on, Ashlinn began to swim, splashing water at him as she kicked and stroked her way past him.

She intended to stay ahead of him, but Flint obviously had his own ideas about that. Soon he was in the lead, and she was following him. He was a faster, stronger swimmer, and she couldn't hope to match his pace.

He kept her in sight, however, frequently looking over his shoulder to make sure she was still in his wake.

Ashlinn was convinced that he wasn't being solicitous because he cared. He was acting dutifully because he was the guide on this expedition and wouldn't want his revered Paradise Outdoors risking a negligence lawsuit were she to drown.

You have this knack of making me want to laugh… I've wanted you every minute of this entire trip. Flint's words echoed in her head as she swam. Enraging her. A good thing too, because otherwise she might very well be crying.

He had said just what she'd needed to hear before sex, and she had been only too willing to believe him. But afterward, having slaked his physical urgency, he hadn't even offered a few token words of—of…

Her thoughts spun off, bitter and inchoate. *What did you want him to say, Ashlinn?* she asked herself derisively. *That you were the best sex he'd ever had? How about "I love you, darling"?* Humiliation washed over her in wave after mortifying wave.

Her muscles ached from the cold, she was exhausted and panting for breath, and she felt as if she'd swallowed half the lake. Still Ashlinn refused to ask Flint to stop and rest. She would not display any signs of weakness to him; she'd done enough of that tonight.

"Do you want to stop?" Flint called to her.

After replaying his voice in her thoughts so many times, the actual sound of it seemed to thunder in her ears. "No!"

"Are you sure?"

She noticed that he didn't stop moving while he asked. Don't do me any favors, she longed to snarl. Except it would take too much energy, and she needed every ounce she possessed to get back to shore under her own power.

"No!" she repeated.

Flint swam on.

He had certainly been eager enough to help her get to the damn sandbar, where he could stand, thus allowing him to have sex with her, Ashlinn fumed, kicking harder. He had held her up, propelling them both through the water, diligently keeping her head above water, so careful to conserve her strength.

But now he'd had her, so there was no reason for him to provide such attention. He kept ahead of her, not even feeling the need to talk to her!

The flashlight lit up the beach like an airport runway, and Ashlinn was inordinately relieved that she'd insisted on wearing her swimsuit to wade into shore. Flint had to endure the embarrassment of striding nude from the water to the rock where he'd cast his jeans.

But he didn't look embarrassed, she noted crossly, as she watched him while dragging herself from the lake. He stood tall and proud and unashamed. His smooth bronze skin, his muscular physique, were highlighted as he walked to the shore.

Ashlinn saw his buttocks, taut and a shade paler than the rest of his skin tone, and her mouth went dry despite all the water she'd swallowed. How strange to have touched him there, sight unseen.

She'd felt him inside her, but seeing him naked for the first time made her blush all over, never mind her shivering goose-flesh and cold purple lips.

Flint had pulled on his jeans and stood waiting as she fumbled with her clothes. Her fingers were numb and clumsy with cold, and what should've taken her only seconds took longer. When she sat down on the rock and began the arduous task of putting on her socks and shoes, he heaved a sigh.

"We'll be here till dawn if you put those on. I'll carry you back to the tent," he declared, and scooped her up in his arms before she could utter a protest.

And protest she did, mightily, once she caught her breath. "Put me down, I can walk, dammit!"

But he refused to listen and marched along the path, holding her over his shoulder, upended like a sack of cement. It was hardly the romantic, cradled-against-his-chest carry celebrated on thousands of book covers and movie posters.

By the time they reached the campsite, Rico, Koji, Bouvier and Jack Hall had all been roused by the commotion and were milling outside their tents. They stared collectively at the water-slick Flint carrying the equally damp, upside-down Ashlinn, who clutched her shoes and socks in her hands.

"What's going on?" asked Rico. "You're both soaked."

Ashlinn bucked and arched and might've kicked, if Flint hadn't set her down on her feet in front of her tent, promptly and efficiently.

"I decided to go for a swim," Ashlinn addressed the puzzled Rico, "and our intrepid guide decided I was drowning and dragged me out of the water." The lie came so easily she surprised herself.

"You're not very grateful to him for saving you." Koji frowned his disapproval.

"Because I'm fine and I didn't need his help. Call it a mistake in the lake," Ashlinn snapped as she crawled into her tent.

She heard the men's voices discussing this latest turn of events, as she pulled off her wet clothes and rubbed her cold skin with a towel.

"She's a stubborn one. And not a very good swimmer either." That was Bouvier. "Good job, Flint."

And from Hall, "What was she thinking, pulling a stunt like that?"

Hot tears warmed Ashlinn's cheeks. A good question, Jack. She stifled a sob. The answer was, she hadn't been thinking at all when she'd pulled a stunt like that.

Six

At his desk by 7:00 a.m., the first to arrive at the office as usual, Flint opened his pocket calendar to the day's date. The second of September.

It had been a month since he'd last seen Ashlinn, a whole month since he had driven her to the Sioux Falls airport where she had boarded her plane for Minneapolis, which would continue on to New York City.

An entire month ago. Longer than the time they'd been together. Still, he'd thought about her every day, as if those two weeks they'd spent in the park had indelibly marked him, holding him in thrall to her.

How long was this going to go on? Flint wondered grimly. He had never been given to obsessive thinking; his mind was too ordered, too disciplined. Or so he'd believed. Mistakenly, it seemed.

Because this past month Ashlinn Carey dominated his thoughts to the point of…obsession? He flinched at the possibility, yet there didn't seem to be anything he could do about it.

He'd certainly tried. As always, work was a welcome panacea, and he extended his already long days at the office, performing his Paradise Outdoors CEO duties par excellence.

But he couldn't live at the company. Eventually, he had to leave and go home—back to his apartment that wasn't a home at all but simply a place of residence.

Where had that maudlin thought come from? Flint wondered dourly. He had never indulged in self-pity in his pre-Ashlinn days. But he was not the same man he had been before meeting Ashlinn. Before making love to her.

Flint stared bleakly at the stark walls of his office.

Pre-Ashlinn, he'd spent the evenings in his apartment reviewing the company's five-year financial goals or debating the merits of Carmody's latest marketing agenda or planning corporate strategy.

Not anymore. Now when he was home alone, his mind focused exclusively on Ashlinn. He might be able to block her out during office hours, but not during the too-long nights.

At night, he walked restlessly through the sparsely furnished rooms of his apartment, trying to hold back the surge of memories that invariably deluged him. He saw Ashlinn laughing, Ashlinn pensive, Ashlinn irritated, exhausted, perplexed, ironic, challenging, baiting, joking, horrified.

Every night, he pictured her every way there was.

In his head, he replayed their conversations about family and work and was startled to realize that he actually recalled the names of all her sisters and brothers, the wholes and the steps, and which was which. He had listened and retained what she'd told him, most unusual for him. He was notoriously inattentive to any nonbusiness related topics, but Ashlinn had never bored him.

He knew irrelevant little details about her that sprang to mind when he least expected: that she loathed eggs and liked plenty of brown sugar sprinkled on her instant oatmeal, that she was drowsy and slow-moving in the early mornings and gulped down at least two cups of strong black coffee, hoping for a jolt of caffeine to deliver its buzz.

That her skin was as smooth and silky-soft to the touch as it looked.

He remembered the unspoken nuances between them. Their shared glances when one of the four adventurers told a chilling or foolhardy tale about the thrills of near-death in dangerous places. Both he and Ashlinn preferred safety to risk-taking. They had admitted and discussed it, very much in sync with each other.

There had been their mutual reluctance to end the late-night camaraderie around the campfire. They were always the last two to call it a night and retire into their tents, lingering just a little bit longer to talk, to laugh together.

Inevitably, the chain of memories would lead to that last night, the one that ended in the lake. To the night of their impulsive lovemaking, which had been the most mind-shattering experience of his life. And not just because it had been great sex, though it certainly had been all that and more.

He'd felt an emotional bond with her that night, a level of unity and acceptance that he had never known with anyone else—except his twin brother. An altogether shocking realization because his relationship with Rafe was certainly far different from his sexual union with Ashlinn.

And it had been a true *union* between Ashlinn and himself. He wasn't deluding himself. Was he?

Flint stopped pacing and gazed out the window at the dark street below.

Was he crazy? He sighed, knowing the answer. He was crazy about Ashlinn Carey, a woman who had made it excruciatingly, painfully clear that she wanted nothing to do with him after making love.

Although she undoubtedly would describe it as simply having sex.

Hot sex. Fantastic sex…

Unable to stop himself, Flint again relived that late-night

tryst in the lake. He and Ashlinn together, her clinging to him as he buried himself deep into her body.

He could hear her cries of pleasure echoing in his head—he had given her much pleasure. When they held each other afterward, replete with satisfaction, it was all he could do to keep himself from telling her he loved her.

It seemed so right—the sex, the love, the words. They all fit together so naturally.

He hadn't said it, though, because the very fact he'd had such a thought stunned him speechless. He had never considered telling a woman he loved her; he'd never been in love before and wasn't willing to lie about it to set a mood.

But this wouldn't have been a lie. He knew it, and the fearsome force of his feelings for Ashlinn sent him reeling. The only strong emotion he knew well was anger, but this...

And then Flint had another thought, one that still had the power to shake him today. *He hadn't used any protection!*

Another first for him, a disturbing, terrifying one. He'd had a few relationships which had progressed to sex, but basically he was too introverted, too quiet, too interested in his work to make much of an effort with women.

Sometimes women pursued him, and if they'd ended up in bed, he had always been meticulously careful to use a condom. He did not want to contract a disease or make a baby. Each was a trap in its own way, and he cherished his independence too much to risk it.

Yet he hadn't given a thought to protection when he and Ashlinn had gone into that lake.

He could use the excuse that he hadn't known she would agree to make love with him, but why bother to delude himself? He'd hoped, he'd wished, he'd wanted...

And when it had actually happened, the furthest thing from his mind was protecting himself from her. Or her from him.

Merging his body with hers had been rapturous, and holding Ashlinn afterward he had been consumed with peace, felt a contentment he hadn't known was possible.

And then the wind had turned colder and she had begun to

shiver in his arms. At that moment, his mind had been reactivated. Panic replaced bliss. Suddenly, his omission struck him, hard.

He hadn't used protection!

Ashlinn hadn't mentioned the lack of it. Should he bring up the subject? What was the protocol in such a situation? Frantic, he made a decision he still questioned today.

He decided the lake was the wrong time and place to talk. Ashlinn was already chilled by the windy water. He didn't want her to risk hypothermia; he wanted to take good care of her.

But from that moment, everything had gone wrong. Everything. When he'd suggested returning to shore, suddenly Ashlinn had turned hostile, taking verbal potshots at him and Paradise Outdoors.

Likening him to a robot!

The moment she had made that remark in cool derision, Flint knew the terrible truth. What he had considered a true union, a mating between kindred souls, she had found unsatisfying. The climax he believed he had given her was only in his imagination. Ashlinn had faked it.

Though not an expert on the sexual Zeitgeist, he was certainly aware that women faked orgasm. And that it was really, really hard to tell the fake from the real thing.

Ashlinn had faked her climax—to please him? to spare his feelings?—sometimes he contemplated her motives but eventually returned to face his failure. He hadn't realized she was faking. Strike one.

Therefore, he hadn't gone on to bring her to completion. Strike two. Finally, with mixed feminine exasperation, frustration and fury, she had given him a hint and called him a robot, daring him to disprove it. To show he was a real man and give her the orgasm she demanded.

He had finally gotten that last one, but hadn't acted on it. Strike three.

Flint winced, remembering how he had withdrawn from her—literally and figuratively—feeling almost sick with pain and humiliation. He should've known not to get too near to a woman as beautiful as Ashlinn Carey, Flint berated himself nightly. He should've stayed clear of a woman who was out of his league when it came to sex, lies and heart smashing.

Compulsively, his thoughts returned to that night. Ashlinn had accused him of being glib—*as if he could conjure up something glib, when he could barely think to speak!*—and proceeded to twist the knife by excelling in the art of flippancy herself.

Still, his concern for her had overridden his hurt. When she'd thrown a tantrum over her missing swimsuit, he had searched the water till he found it floating, all the while enduring her attacks on his company.

He had protectively kept her in sight during their swim to shore despite Ashlinn's determination to keep her distance from him. He'd carried her back to her tent because she was cold and fatigued, though touching her had been torture for him.

He still wanted her madly and she had made it plain that she loathed him.

Even worse was the cool little lie she had spouted so easily to the others at the campsite. Her words conveyed a bitter rebuke, one he took to heart. She didn't need him, she didn't want him. She'd said so, reviling the "mistake in the lake."

Mistake in the lake. How could he initiate the lack-of-protection discussion with her after hearing that? Yet how could he say nothing about it at all?

Angry and hurt, he'd lain awake in his tent rehearsing what to say and how to say it to her, but by daybreak, he'd had a revelation. Maybe Ashlinn hadn't mentioned his lack of a condom because she'd used protection herself? Maybe she was on the pill or something?

He hadn't gotten the opportunity to ask her, because they weren't alone for even a moment the next day, not during the long drive to Sioux Falls or at the airport. Plus, Ashlinn's icy demeanor made her unapproachable. There were rattlesnakes at the Great Plains Zoo less forbidding than Ms. Carey on that particular day.

Eva later told him that there were all kinds of new devices

on the prophylactic market now, like a female condom. The very mention of such a thing stymied Flint. *A female condom?* Whoever had heard of that?

Eva had, and she ought to know since she'd already completed her Ob-Gyn rotation in med school. Eva also mentioned the Emergency Contraceptive Kit, which included a dosage of birth control pills designed to prevent pregnancy up to seventy-two hours after unprotected sex. Eva insisted that all sophisticated women were well acquainted with such items, that such a woman would take charge of her sexuality without depending on a man.

That particular conversation he'd had with his younger sister still made Flint sweat. He had tried to be subtle, to speak in generalities about a hypothetical situation, but Eva was sharp. He sensed that she'd guessed something had happened between him and the beautiful woman who'd been along on the Paradise Outdoors camping expedition.

Well, something had definitely happened. And Ashlinn was sophisticated, living and working in New York, just like that hypothetical woman whom Eva assured him would "take charge of her sexuality and protect herself."

It stood to reason that Ashlinn had done what Eva said. It was also reasonable to assume that, based on her actions and by what she'd said and left unsaid, Ashlinn wanted nothing further to do with him. Reasonable but so damn painful!

So Flint tried to resign himself to never seeing Ashlinn again. He worked to convince himself that his passionate interlude with her couldn't have resulted in any little consequences. That she would contact him, if she felt the need or the urge, if she ever wanted to see him again.

Two weeks later, when the phone rang at his apartment one night at eleven o'clock, he raced to snatch the receiver. No one ever called him at home at this hour. Could it possibly be...?

"Hey, Flint." The voice of his youngest half sister, Kaylin, sounded in his ear.

Flint nearly dropped the phone in disappointment. "Hello, Kaylin."

"Don't sound so happy to hear from me," she said sarcastically, and then rushed ahead, her voice high with excitement. "Flint, will you go to New York? To New York City, I mean."

"What?" He sat down hard on the sofa, his fingers clenched.

"It's really, really important, Flint. Camryn is there. 'Cause she quit college."

"Quit? She just got there a week and a half ago." Flint had been summoned to dinner at Rafe and Holly's house to say goodbye to Camryn the night before she left for the university in Vermillion. He didn't expect the kid to set the academic world on fire but quitting this soon surprised even him.

And then it struck him, "Why are you calling me, Kaylin? What did Rafe…"

"Rafe doesn't know yet," Kaylin cut in. "And he doesn't have to ever know, either. I think we can talk Camryn into going back to school and we won't have to tell Rafe and Holly. They would just be worried sick," she added dramatically. "So will you go to New York tomorrow and talk to Camryn. Okay, Flint? Please!"

"New York City," Flint murmured. His mind was spinning in a kaleidoscope whirl. He tried to focus. "Why did Camryn go there, Kaylin?"

"Who knows why Camryn does anything?"

That was certainly true. Those kids were a total mystery to him. "I take it Camryn has called you and told you where she is in the city."

"Yeah." Kaylin told him the address, and he wrote it down.

"I'll leave tomorrow and bring the little fiend back," Flint said decisively.

He smiled, for the first time in six weeks. He was going to New York. Doing a good deed, retrieving his devilish half sister, sparing Rafe and Holly all that worry. And while he was in the city, he might just look up Ashlinn Carey.

Strictly on a professional basis, of course. He hadn't heard a word about her article for *Tour & Travel* or when it would appear; the information would be useful for ordering, stocking and pricing in future catalogs.

He repeated that like a mantra as he flew to New York.

The *Tour & Travel* office was sheer pandemonium when Ashlinn arrived, which was nothing new.

Chaos had reigned since Junior's departure a month ago, when he had decided he was tired of the publishing business in general and *Tour & Travel* in particular. His latest goal was to make films, and shortly after Ashlinn's return from South Dakota he had left the office and not returned. Rumor had it he was currently in Canada for the Toronto Film Festival "to network with the players in the industry."

Meanwhile, there was anarchy at the magazine. Next month's issue wasn't on the boards, and even Junior's indulgent father realized that something had to be done. Presley Oakes Sr. had personally asked Ashlinn to take charge during his son's absence, acknowledging that she was the only one there with experience in putting out a magazine. He'd also offered her a raise to go along with her new responsibilities.

Too bad Junior's handpicked staff didn't acknowledge her authority. Their collective incompetence and/or indifference dogged her every step of the way. Coming into the office each day was migraine-inducing, with irate advertisers to placate, infuriated writers to soothe and the young staff of underachievers to motivate.

Still, there had been a time when she might've been able to handle it all, to cope and succeed, maybe even turn the mayhem into the opportunity of a lifetime.

Ashlinn knew that her old self certainly would've given it her best shot. Unfortunately, her current self was too preoccupied, too terrified, too utterly heartbroken, to think much about the travails of *Tour & Travel*. This morning she'd arrived at the office later than anybody else, succumbing to the lack of discipline that plagued everybody else around here.

Ashlinn didn't care. Last night she had finally and irrevocably faced the truth; she couldn't pretend any longer.

She was absolutely, positively pregnant.

She, Ashlinn Carey, who had once felt confident enough about her own knowledge and power to write *Hooked!*, a book in which she took to task women addicted to the wrong men, was pregnant by a man who had used her sexually but had no further interest in her. Even before she'd known she was pregnant, she couldn't get Flint out of her head—*he'd* hooked *her*. There seemed to be some kind of cosmic irony at work, perhaps a dark joke, but Ashlinn couldn't appreciate either.

That night in the lake with Flint Paradise had left its indelible mark in her body, on her life, but he didn't care about her at all. Their lovemaking had been a spur-of-the-moment mistake to him. He'd made that painfully clear by his dismissive behavior that night, and even more agonizingly, by his telling six-week silence.

She was no different from those hapless women she'd chronicled in *Hooked!*—waiting, hoping, even praying that Flint would call her. Any excuse would do. Ashlinn knew she would have been so happy to hear from him that she'd have forgiven him anything, just to hear his voice, to know that he cared about her even a little.

But Flint hadn't called.

When her period was ten days late—an unheard-of lapse in her always regular cycle—she had geared up her courage and bought a pregnancy test kit at the drugstore. She'd passed—or failed—depending on one's point of view.

The test was positive.

Yet aside from the missed period, she hadn't had any other signs or symptoms of pregnancy. There was no nausea, fatigue, weight gain or food cravings such as Michelle and Courtney had described during their pregnancies.

Ashlinn realized how easy it was to delude oneself into thinking that the condition just wasn't real. That the test had been mistaken, her missed period simply a fluke. To prove it, yesterday she'd bought another brand of test, almost convincing herself that the results would be different.

They weren't, of course. Ashlinn finally dropped the last

vestige of denial and faced reality. It was a tough moment, a harsh truth. She was pregnant with Flint Paradise's child, and the father of her baby had undoubtedly forgotten all about her. And to top it all off, she was working in the office from hell.

Ashlinn didn't allow herself to cry, although she wanted to— badly. The stronger her urge to weep, the tighter the control she exerted to hold herself in check. She didn't cry, but she spent most of the night tossing and turning, her mind racing from panic to fury to sorrow and back again, repeating the cycle over and over.

When she finally fell into a fitful troubled sleep, her dreams mirrored her thoughts. Ashlinn jerked awake, trembling and tearful.

What was she going to do? She was one month pregnant. One down, eight to go. The countdown dazed her. She was going to have a baby.

What was she going to do?

And now this morning, after a lurching stop-and-start bus ride in the rain through near-gridlock traffic, Ashlinn entered the office to find the young staffers behaving like a class whose teacher had called in sick and who had no intention of behaving for the unlucky substitute stuck in charge.

Which was nothing new. Every morning was like this. But today Ashlinn felt simultaneously nauseated and ravenous, and she couldn't face it.

"Don't put any calls through to me," she ordered Junior's assistant Shawna, whose plans included either becoming a supermodel or marrying Junior.

Shawna looked up from her copy of *Allure* magazine and shrugged. "Okay."

"I'll be in Jun—uh—Mr. Oakes's office. Don't let anyone in, I don't want to be disturbed," Ashlinn added, entering Junior's custom-designed-only-to-be-abandoned office.

Though she'd been put in charge, she had remained at her own desk, opting to avoid her young boss's private domain. Now she decided to make it her sanctuary, a place to think and recover from her upset stomach before attempting to face the frenzied world of *Tour & Travel.*

Standing on the sidewalk in the drizzling rain, a perplexed Flint glanced at the address he had written down, then took another look at the building in the middle of the busy New York block.

What was Camryn doing here, in what was clearly an office building in midtown Manhattan?

The raindrops came harder and faster, pelting him. Automatically, Flint entered the building to escape them.

He strode to the elevators, quickly stepping into a full car whose doors were just closing. Camryn was supposed to be on the fourteenth floor. Flint hit the button marked fourteen, despite his growing doubts. His fellow passengers were all wearing working attire, and at every floor people got off, heading to what were definitely offices.

Maybe there was some kind of non-profit humanitarian organization housed here, one that dealt with youngsters who'd arrived in the city with no resources? Of course, demonic little Camryn was extremely resourceful, Flint mused grimly. New York was probably more at risk from her than the other way round.

Thinking of his rebellious kid sister was a useful diversion, keeping him from wondering what kind of reception he would get from Ashlinn when he went to her apartment later today. He'd worked out a plan—to arrive around dinner time, when, presumably, she would be home from work and hungry, and to suggest taking her out to eat.

The plan required her to accept his invitation, and Flint didn't let himself take the scenario any further. His imagination had already concocted too many hair-raising ones.

During the endless trip to New York—which had included a delayed flight, a change of planes and half an hour of circling La Guardia—he had envisioned himself arriving at her apartment door and Ashlinn refusing to open it to him; calling the police when he tried to talk to her.

In an alternate, even worse, version, he pictured Ashlinn flinging open the door and screaming, cursing him, attacking him like a vicious she-wolf. Somehow in his mind's eye, she had been morphed into his father's odious second wife Marcine, the woman who'd made the wicked stepmother of fairy-tale fame her role model; the woman who had been so cold and cruel to him and Rafe and Eva while making their father's life a living hell.

Thankfully, the image of Marcine quickly dissolved, replaced by another of Ashlinn. He yearned for her, but after her resounding six-week silence, there was a very real possibility that she wouldn't want to see him. He needed a back-up plan.

In a nervous sweat, Flint conceded that he might have to ask Camryn for help, after he'd retrieved her. "Desperate times call for desperate measures"; he recalled that quote from somewhere. Well, he was desperate, and Camryn excelled in scheming and manipulation. He only hoped she was amenable to bribes, because he could think of no other way to obtain her assistance.

The elevator stopped at the fourteenth floor and the doors snapped open. Flint emerged from the car and headed left, following an arrow down a long corridor.

He stopped dead in front of the door with *Tour & Travel* lettered on the glass. No, it couldn't be. Camryn wouldn't have come here.

His heart began to thud, the beat echoing like a bass drum in his ears. The girl was unpredictable, but why would she run away to the magazine where Ashlinn Carey worked?

Could he have possibly gotten the address wrong? It would be a bizarre coincidence, but no, Flint rejected that possibility. He knew he had written down exactly what he'd heard. This was where Kaylin had directed him. Bratty Kaylin, who was as devious as her sister...

He decided to leave; he needed time to regain his composure, to rethink the situation and plan his next move.

"Come on in," a young man dressed all in black opened the door, as if expecting him.

Too off-balance and off-guard not to, Flint followed the young man inside.

"Hey, where's the stuff?" demanded the man in black and Flint stared at him blankly.

"He's not from the deli, you idiot," a young woman scolded her colleague, giving Flint a cursory once-over, taking in his gray suit, starched white shirt and sedate striped tie. "You probably want to see the boss. Straight that way." She pointed to a closed door at the far side of the cavernous cubicle-filled office.

Flint stared around him as he headed toward that door. None of these people were wearing appropriate office attire and he could tell at a glance that this was not an orderly, productive workplace. He frowned his disapproval, remembering Ashlinn's complaints. From what he could see, she had understated the situation.

He stopped in front of the publisher's office door and knocked twice. There was no response. From the noise level around him, it was safe to assume his knock hadn't been heard. Boldly, Flint opened the door, an action he wouldn't have taken anywhere but here, where normal office etiquette obviously was not practiced.

"When in Rome," he counseled himself and stepped inside. His feet seemed to sink on a carpet so thick and plush, it was like stepping into a field of marshmallows.

He stopped in his tracks at the sight of the dark-haired young woman sitting behind the most enormous desk he'd ever seen.

"Ashlinn!"

Her head jerked up at the sound of his voice, and for just a moment, her face lit, her eyes widened and brightened as they met his. And then her expression changed, became cool and guarded. She directed her gaze to somewhere over his left shoulder and rose to her feet, bracing her palms on the desktop in front of her.

"If you've come to see Presley Oakes Jr., he isn't here."

Flint looked at her hungrily, taking in every detail. The thick, dark luxuriant hair that tumbled around her shoulders. The beautiful face he had seen daily in his dreams and his waking hours, too.

She was wearing a black-and-blue floral-print dress that would've been considered too short for office wear in Sioux Falls, but compared to some of the getups he'd seen on the *Tour & Travel* staffers in the outer office, actually looked conservative. His eyes lingered for a moment on the soft curve of her breasts.

Her icy tone, coupled with her don't-come-a-step-closer expression and body language, radiated hostility and rejection, and if he hadn't caught that one brief but distinct flash of joy when she'd first seen him, Flint knew he would've considered himself persona non grata and probably acted accordingly.

But what he had read in her face and her eyes empowered him. "I'm not here to see Junior." He backtracked, closed and locked the office door. Then he strolled toward the oversized desk, his eyes never leaving her.

He stopped when he came to the edge of the desk.

Ashlinn gulped for breath. Her palms were sweating. She didn't dare lift them from the surface of the desk because they would probably leave damp prints, evidence of how very nervous she was.

"Do you want me to leave?" Flint asked, already walking around the desk, coming closer and closer to her.

Ashlinn caught a glimpse of the two of them in the enormous mirror that lined one wall of the office. Her own expression stunned her. She was staring at Flint with the same rapture that she'd seen on the faces of preteen girls standing in line to see *Titanic*.

No wonder he didn't hesitate in his approach! His question had been merely a token; he already knew her answer. Flint Paradise fairly radiated the confidence and sexual power she had given him by her dreamy-eyed, come-hither gaze. Oh, yes, he knew very well how much she wanted him.

The very thought caused a revealing moisture to pool at her center. Ashlinn flushed crimson. *I'm not here to see Junior.* His words rang in her ears. Which meant he had come to see her. And if the look on her face gave her away, Flint's was equally easy to read. He wanted her.

Yet now that he was finally here after six interminable weeks, now that she was finally feeling secure since it was obvious he'd come to see her, Ashlinn felt a rebellious spark. She had been so miserable, so scared!

Why should she make this easy for him?

Flint's hands closed over her arms and he pulled her close. Ashlinn impacted against him with a sensual thud, and she felt its effects in every erogenous zone in her body.

"Tell me you want me to stay, Ashlinn," Flint commanded, his mouth brushing hers.

Seven

Ashlinn had no intention of obeying him. But Flint smoothed his hands down the length of her arms, and she reflexively raised them as he clasped her around the waist.

"Hello, Ashlinn." His voice was husky and deep and his dark eyes held hers. His fingers kneaded her waist, arching her into him.

"Do you think you can just waltz in here and make demands after six weeks without a single word?"

Ashlinn intended to sound blasé and breezy. A bit of amused laughter might have helped her achieve that effect, but she couldn't pull it off. Nor could she draw her gaze from his. Her hands rested on his shoulders and she stared up at him, lost in his eyes.

No, she was definitely not playing it cool. How could she when her senses were filled with him? The fresh scent of his aftershave, the hard warmth of his body pressed close to hers, were irresistible.

"I think I can." He teased her mouth with his lips, his teeth, his tongue. "Because you're letting me."

"You're a thoughtless jerk, Flint Paradise."

Spoken in a soft, almost caressive tone, it wasn't much of an invective. But Ashlinn couldn't help her lack of ire. She was so glad to see him, so thrilled to be back in his arms. And so relieved that he'd come to her.

That didn't mean she was simply going to excuse him, however. Not after he'd ignored her for six endless weeks.

"I don't approve of drop-in visitors, especially not in the workplace," she admonished. Standing on tiptoe and nuzzling his neck as she spoke definitely took the sting out of her rebuke.

But Flint's body tensed. "If I'd called first, would you have seen me, Ashlinn?"

She drew back a little and searched his face. He met her eyes, his expression unreadable. "What do you think?" Ashlinn asked warily.

"So the ball's back in my court?" Flint heaved a sigh. "Damn, I hate these games."

"I'm not playing a game." That sounded too much like an admission. Or maybe a plea. Ashlinn frowned. "Just answer the question, Flint. And not with one of your own."

"Okay, here goes..." He seemed to take a mental deep breath. "I didn't think you wanted to see me or to hear from me, Ashlinn. So I didn't risk it."

Ashlinn was astounded. Was this a line or did he actually believe she hadn't wanted to hear from him? "You didn't risk it," she echoed.

"I don't handle rejection well. Never have. I avoid the chance of it, in personal situations. A business risk is different, of course."

"Of course." Being Flint, he had to clarify his position in regard to Paradise Outdoors. Ashlinn knew she must be ready to forgive him when she found his precision endearing rather than irritating.

"I don't go looking for personal rejection myself," she

added, thinking of *Hooked!*, her sermon to those hapless women who clung to men, despite the most blatant rejections. She'd never feared becoming one of them; she had made it a point to do the rejecting first.

It seemed that Flint did too, which had brought them to an impasse—until now. His confession freed something within her.

"I didn't think you wanted to hear from me either," she said slowly, cautiously.

They looked at each other for one long charged moment.

"You couldn't be more wrong, Ashlinn."

He gathered her close and opened his mouth over hers in a fiercely possessive kiss.

With a small sigh, she welcomed his tongue, clinging to him, as searing flames of sensual heat licked through her. The taste of him was heady, and Ashlinn threaded her fingers through his hair, returning his kiss with hungry ardor.

She was starving for him, needing him, craving him with her whole being. She had to be part of him again, joined with him in the most elemental way. Ashlinn let him know it, holding nothing back.

One drugging kiss merged into another, each deeper and more intense, building in passion and urgency. His big hand closed over one breast, seeking her turgid nipple. Ashlinn winced at the unexpected discomfort. Within the past few weeks, her breasts had become particularly tender, her nipples sore and painfully sensitive to even the light touch of her clothing. Flint's erotic little pinch made her jump.

Instantly attuned to her, he lifted his mouth from hers. "Ashlinn, did I hurt you?" He stared down at her with black eyes filled with concern.

To Ashlinn's dismay, tears pricked her eyes. Not from pain, but from a sudden surge of emotion. It was happening more and more these days, the rush of tears inspired by almost anything, be it sad, touching, funny or even sappy. Knowing her volatile emotional swings were caused by the elevating hormone levels of pregnancy didn't stop them. Staying in control was becoming more and more difficult.

"I'm fine," she whispered, trying to turn her head.

She didn't dare lose control around Flint. The last time she'd done that had been in a South Dakota lake and she'd ended up pregnant—a pregnancy Flint was unaware of. Ashlinn squeezed her eyes shut in an attempt to keep the tears from spilling out and down her cheeks.

Flint caught her chin between his thumb and forefinger, holding her in place. "You're crying!" He sounded horror-stricken.

The urge to indulge in a full-fledged fit of weeping here in his arms shocked Ashlinn out of her tears. She couldn't give into such foolish impulses!

She rallied, gulping back a sob. "I'm not crying."

His index finger brushed her cheek, following the track of a tear. "No?"

If only he'd been sarcastic, lamented Ashlinn, if only he'd challenged her, determined to wring an admission from her. Her fighting spirit would have been revived, and she could've held out against him. But Flint's tone was warm and sympathetic, inspiring her to cuddle closer instead of pushing him away.

He smoothed his hand over her hair. "I was too rough. I'm sorry, Ashlinn."

"You weren't. It's—me."

"You're so sensitive. Ultra sensitive." He leaned his forehead against hers. "I remember that, I remember how it was between us, Ashlinn. I remember everything. I've thought about you constantly."

His other hand glided over the curve of her hip and down the outside of her thigh. Ashlinn trembled.

"I want to see you," he murmured, his voice, his lips seductive as he kissed a path along the curve of her neck. "That night in the lake…it was dark and I didn't really see you. I've spent the past six weeks imagining…"

She felt him lift the skirt of her dress, pushing it up as he slid his palm higher on her leg. Ashlinn closed her eyes and leaned into him, a soft moan escaping from her throat.

"I missed you, Ashlinn. And I want you so much." His hand moved over her bottom, pausing to knead the firm rounded curves. When she didn't draw away, when she continued to cling to him, he slipped his hand between her thighs.

She gasped weakly as he began to caress her there.

"You want me, too," he said hoarsely. She arched helplessly against his tantalizing fingers, and he caressed her with potent, possessive intimacy. "You're so wet and hot and I can feel how much you want me, Ashlinn."

A wild surge of longing ripped through her. It was as if her body had been primed and ready for him. She wanted sex and she wanted it now. With Flint, of course. She wanted only him. The ferocity of her arousal shook her.

Her changing body seemed foreign to her, its needs unpredictable. Did pregnancy heighten a woman's desire for the man whose child she carried? Flint had kissed her and touched her and told her that he wanted her, and now she was all set to forget the past six weeks of silence, to forget he wasn't aware that she was pregnant. To even forget they were in Junior's office and the *Tour & Travel* staff were just outside the door!

Long-ingrained notions of propriety abruptly surfaced. "Flint, we can't." She laid her hands on his forearms.

Flint went still. "You're right."

Slowly, he withdrew his hand from between her legs, letting her skirt slide back into place. He had some of his own long-ingrained notions of propriety to pacify. "Not here," he added grudgingly. "After all, it *is* a place of business."

Ashlinn grinned. She couldn't help herself. "You say that with the same reverence as 'house of worship.'"

Flint returned her smile, and she felt her heart soar. He didn't smile often, so when he did, it was a dazzling treat.

"Let's get out of here," urged Flint. "Right now."

"You're suggesting that I take an early lunch hour?"

"Yeah, combined with an extended coffee break, several of them. That should get us to five o'clock. Quitting time."

Picking up their camping expedition camaraderie was easy. Ashlinn was pleased that Flint obviously felt the same.

She tilted her head, playfully, seductively. "Is that the way you do business in South Dakota? Office hours are about an hour in the morning, from around ten to eleven?"

"Yeah, baby. That's exactly how it is." His exaggerated reassurance was intended to make her laugh, and it did.

"You forget I saw you run Paradise Outdoors from the outdoors. Even in the middle of the woods you managed to put in hours of work."

"True." Flint cleared his throat. "I'm an admitted workaholic, but lately I've come to the conclusion that there might be more to life than work."

"That is a shocking conclusion, coming from Flint Paradise," she said lightly.

"More like blasphemy. But there it is, Ashlinn."

"Poor Flint." She fiddled with Junior's elaborate pen collection, not meeting Flint's gaze. "There's nothing like having your worldview turned on its head to make you feel a few—a few—" she fumbled around with the items on Junior's desk, looking for a cleverly apt analogy. Her voice trailed off. She was totally out of cleverly apt analogies.

"A few staples short of a staple gun?" Flint suggested helpfully, picking up Junior's high-tech one that resembled a weapon from *Star Wars.*

Ashlinn rolled her eyes.

Flint was undaunted. "Seems as if you know what I'm talking about, Ashlinn, hmm?" His dark eyes, his tone were challenging. "As if you know what it's been like these past six weeks."

"You have no idea," she mumbled.

Now would be the time to mention something about how *she* had spent the past six weeks. To bring up the anxieties of a missed period, the apprehension of buying a pregnancy test kit. Not to mention the poignant terror of learning you were pregnant by a man you thought didn't care enough about you even to pick up the telephone and say hello.

Yes, she knew what it felt like to be…a few staples short of a staple gun!

"Don't." Suddenly, Flint pulled her firmly against him.

"Don't what?" She felt the insistence of his hard body, the need that wouldn't be denied.

"Get all tense." He cupped her cheek, raising her face to him. "Like you're doing right now. You're ramrod straight, stiff as a broomstick."

"What do you expect?" Ashlinn was appalled that her tears had made an unwelcome, unexpected comeback. How could she tell him she was pregnant?

No, she couldn't tell him, she just couldn't! "You—you insult me, compare me to a staple gun and then a broomstick. Oh, I get your allusions, all right: broomstick—witch. Staple gun—" she swallowed. "Actually, that particular allusion eludes me, but I know you meant it to be insulting."

"Honey, you credit me with way too much imagination." Flint scooped her up in his arms and carried her toward the door.

"What are you…put me down!" exclaimed Ashlinn, her weepiness careening into panic. "Flint, no!"

Held high against his chest, she felt the strength in his muscular arms, the heat of his big hands under her thighs. She remembered the way he'd carried her after their fateful swim in the lake, flung over his shoulder like a sack of dirty laundry. But now he'd turned romantic, and the gesture threatened to completely demolish her defenses.

And she had to keep them up. If she were to slip…

"Please put me down, Flint." She sounded desperate, she *was* desperate.

"I don't want to." Flint paused at the door, in front of the giant mirror. Their reflections stared back at them. Her head seemed to rest naturally against the solid breadth of his chest, and his eyes burned into hers.

"We—can't always get what we want," she said breathlessly.

"Now why did I know you were going to say something

like that?'' Flint actually laughed. ''Probably because it's something I might've said—before my worldview was turned on its head, that is.''

''You mean before you turned Neanderthal.'' Ashlinn scowled. ''Put me down right now, Flint.''

Her double in the mirror was scowling, too. But the softness in her eyes and the way her body snuggled into Flint's totally negated her demand. No wonder he felt free to dismiss it.

''Your boss has strange taste in office decor. A mirror for a wall might work in a Nevada brothel or something, but it's really bizarre for an office,'' Flint observed, in what was clearly a diversionary tactic.

Even realizing it, Ashlinn went along with the ploy. They needed a neutral topic, a time-out from their incipient argument, if that's what it was. ''A—a wall-sized mirror is essential for a narcissist like Junior who enjoys watching his own every move.''

It felt surreal to be discussing Junior, to be looking at the couple in the mirror—who appeared to be fascinated with each other even though they were ostensibly discussing Junior and mirrors and narcissism.

But most of all, it felt good being with Flint. Why bother to fight it? she mused dizzily. She was where she wanted to be.

''If I'd thought you wanted to see me, I would've taken the first plane to New York, Ashlinn.'' Flint set her on her feet, letting her slide slowly down the length of him, turning the release into a long caress.

Ashlinn's body throbbed with arousal. ''Are you apologizing for waiting so long to…''

''Yes, I am. I'm apologizing for everything, Ashlinn.'' He sounded as desperate as she had a few moments ago.

''When a man is desperate for sex, he'll say anything, especially if he thinks it's what a woman wants to hear,'' she murmured in a faraway voice.

''Are you throwing my apology back in my face?'' Flint's face hardened. ''That's unfair, Ashlinn.''

''I wasn't talking about you, Flint. I was just remembering

that's what I said to my stepsister Michelle when she told me that Steve, the man she ended up marrying, told her that he loved her.'' Ashlinn looked troubled. ''I said all it meant was that he was desperate for sex. I thought I was so perceptive, but it was really just plain awful of me, wasn't it?''

''Cynical, maybe, but you meant well, Ashlinn.'' The edge of anger was gone from Flint's voice. ''You were only trying to help,'' he added soothingly, wrapping his arms around her waist and pulling her back against his long hard frame.

''Some help!'' Just picturing Michelle's face that day made Ashlinn feel like crying. She hadn't thought about it in a long time, but the memory suddenly reappeared, sharp and fresh, as if it had happened yesterday. ''How could I have been so heartless?''

''It's no worse than me telling my brother that the woman he loved was in cahoots with our half sisters to sabotage Paradise Outdoors. Or that Holly was merely faking an interest in the kids because she wanted to trap Rafe into impregnating her.'' Flint shook his head ruefully. ''Yeah, I also told him that.''

''Michelle and Steve love each other. They have one-year-old twins, a boy and a girl, and they're genuinely happy,'' Ashlinn wailed. ''I was so wrong about them, Flint.''

''It's not a crime to be wrong, honey. I was wrong about Holly and Rafe, too. After all, the company wasn't sabotaged and Holly's not pregnant, thank God. She and Rafe want to wait a while before they have kids, which is extremely wise and sensible. That's why I'm finally convinced they have a real chance of making it last between them.''

He thought it was sensible and wise not to have children? Flint's words seemed to bounce around in Ashlinn's head, reverberating like the Voice of Doom. Her mouth felt dry, as if stuffed with cotton.

''My dad and his second wife Marcine got married after knowing each other only a short time, just like Rafe and Holly, but the similarity ends there,'' continued Flint. ''Dad and Marcine had Camryn ten months after they married and Kaylin arrived just twelve months later. What a catastrophe that turned out to be!''

"Catastrophe?'' Ashlinn repeated weakly. *He described having children as a catastrophe!*

"Marcine disappeared with the girls when they were one and two years old, and Dad died without ever seeing them again.'' Flint grimaced. ''They didn't surface till they were teenagers, when they came to Sioux Falls to live with Rafe after their mother's death.''

"I—I don't know what to say,'' Ashlinn managed. Flint's anti-child revelations had all but rendered her speechless.

"It probably sounds harsh but Rafe and Eva and I were glad when Marcine was gone. Not Dad, though, he took it hard.'' Flint shrugged. ''If only Dad had put off having those kids, he'd have seen early on that Marcine was a menace with a heart of stone. Would have saved himself a helluva lot of heartbreak, not to mention sparing Rafe getting stuck with the little troublemakers. It's a life sentence for him.''

Ashlinn flinched. If Flint thought a married couple should wait a long time before committing themselves to what he considered the catastrophe of children, an out-of-wedlock pregnancy must top the list of his horror of horrors. *He viewed children as a life sentence, like prison!*

Unconsciously, she laid her hand on her abdomen. She recognized the protective gesture for what it was, a fledgling maternal bond with her unborn child—whose own father considered it a catastrophe.

Not that she had been a paragon of parental devotion, Ashlinn admitted to herself, feeling ashamed. When it came to joyfully anticipating this child, she had definitely been remiss.

She thought of how badly her brother Mark and his wife Marianne had wanted children; their infertility had broken their hearts. The couple had eventually adopted an orphaned sibling group, but the ease with which she had conceived Flint's baby provided a stark contrast to Mark and Marianne's insurmountable difficulties.

Did people always want what they didn't have? Ashlinn wondered bleakly. Or *not* want what they could have? She made a fervent, heartfelt promise to herself to cherish this innocent little baby, unwanted by its father.

Flint began to nibble on her neck. Ashlinn watched the erotic scene in the mirror as she felt the sensuous pressure of his lips, the provocative nip of his teeth.

"I have a hotel room, Ashlinn. Will you come with me?" His black eyes glittered with desire.

If she went with him, it would be for this one last time, Ashlinn acknowledged achingly. Because after today, she had to end their relationship.

She now knew for certain that she could never tell Flint about the baby she was carrying. He didn't want it; he'd all but confirmed that already. He would consider her a conniving menace with a heart of stone and hate her for foisting an unplanned, unwelcome child on him, for disrupting his life.

Perhaps the late Ben Paradise had regretted Marcine's departure with the two baby girls, but Flint certainly hadn't. His attitude had been one of "good riddance." Ashlinn decided she would save him the trouble of rejecting their own baby— and save herself the trauma of seeing it happen—by keeping from him any knowledge of their child's existence. She and her baby weren't going to be any man's life sentence!

In the mirror, Ashlinn saw the shine of tears in her eyes and determinedly blinked them away. Meanwhile, would it be so very wrong to make love with Flint one final time? She'd missed him so much, she'd wanted him so much.

She needed him.

And she had been without him for six whole weeks. Now he was here holding her, wanting her. The temptation was strong, too strong for her to overcome.

Ashlinn couldn't resist—not Flint or her own feelings for him.

"Yes, Flint." Ashlinn reached up and stroked his cheek. There was a lump in her throat and she swallowed convulsively. "I'll go to your hotel with you."

* * *

"If it keeps raining like this, we'll have to build an ark to get around," grumbled Flint. He and Ashlinn stood inside the foyer of her office building while rain fell in sheets outside. "What is it about us and rain, anyway? Remember that first night in the park when—"

"The bus stop is right down the street," Ashlinn interjected. "The buses are going to be crowded so we'd better—"

"A bus? No thanks, we'll take a taxi," Flint said decisively.

"Says the out-of-towner." Ashlinn rolled her eyes at his naive optimism. "We'll never get a taxi in this rain. There aren't enough cabs in the city to meet the demand in bad weather."

"So you're calmly resigned to waiting for an overcrowded bus? Well, I'm not."

Moments later, he spied a taxi and dashed into the street, expertly dodging the slow-moving, near-gridlocked traffic, to hail the cabbie with all the expertise of a native New Yorker.

"I'm impressed," Ashlinn admitted. "It's as if you conjured up this taxi and then beat out everybody else for it."

They were cozily ensconced in the back seat, secluded from the pounding rain and drenched pedestrians.

"I'm your Paradise Outdoors guide, remember? Taking care of you is my duty. On second thought, let me rephrase that...." Flint made his move, sliding his arm around her and drawing her closer to him. "It's my pleasure, Ashlinn."

Ashlinn automatically stiffened. She wasn't accustomed to being handled, and even though it was Flint, her reflexes immediately kicked in.

Flint noticed. "Let's not go through the whole broomstick-staple gun thing again." His hand cupped her cheek, stroked it. "Relax, Ashlinn. That's it," he murmured as her tension began to dissolve and she slowly leaned into him, letting his hard frame support her.

He lowered his head, his lips mere centimeters from hers. "I can't wait any longer to kiss you," he confessed huskily. "It took all my willpower to chastely escort you out of your building. It's too much to expect me to sit here with you and not…''

"What about our audience?" Ashlinn whispered, feeling inhibited. "The driver keeps sneaking glances at us in the rearview mirror."

"He's just listening to his radio," Flint spoke loud enough for the driver to hear. A second later, the radio volume was turned up loud, the announcer's voice filling the cab, sharp and shrill.

"*Now* he's just listening to his radio. Very subtle, Flint."

Flint chuckled, unrepentant. "What language is that anyway?"

"I have no idea, it's not even remotely familiar. But I bet Bouvier or Koji or Hall or Rico could pick out a few phrases," Ashlinn murmured dryly. Her head rested comfortably in the hollow of Flint's shoulder. "Probably something like 'And now, live from Diyarbakir.'"

"Or Diredawa," Flint joined in the game. "Did you ever get a copy of *The Most Dangerous Places on the Globe*?"

"Soon as I got home, I bought and read it. They're dangerous places, all right, and I still don't want to go to any of them."

"Were our campmates mentioned, like they said?"

"Oh yes, all four names were listed in the Acknowledgments. I've exchanged e-mail with them since I got back to New York. They like me a whole lot better when I'm thousands of miles away from them, not diluting any potential adventures."

"I haven't heard from any of them." Flint felt one of those irrational pangs of jealousy at the thought of Ashlinn communicating with the other four when he hadn't heard a single word from her. "And to set the record straight, they liked you very much the whole time we were camping."

"How soon you forget." Ashlinn laughed. "Those guys considered me a burden at worst, a pest at best, and were delighted to consign me to you."

"I was delighted to have you. And I'm sick of talking about the fearless four."

He *had* to kiss her. If he didn't he would surely implode!

His lips touched hers in a succession of quick feather-light kisses. At first, Ashlinn didn't respond, and he thought she was going to pull away or else push him away from her.

He didn't intend to let that happen.

Flint held his ground, continuing the light kisses, neither increasing nor decreasing the gentle pressure. His technique was successful. Within a few moments, Ashlinn's hands moved to his chest. The fingers of one hand curled around the material of his shirt; she slid the fingertips of her other hand between the buttons, seeking bare skin. Finding it.

She sighed softly against his mouth, and the sensuous little sound shot straight to his groin. With a groan, Flint pulled her hard against him, anchoring her there with one arm around her waist, his other hand clasping the nape of her neck.

Her lips parted, permitting him entry, and he responded with the slow slide of his tongue, sensuously rubbing hers, stroking, filling her mouth. He felt her body relax against his, and he deepened the kiss.

It was erotically tantalizing, necking in the back seat of a taxi, Flint mused dazedly. They were constrained by the presence of the driver from going any further than deepening their kisses, from holding each other closer and tighter.

Yet the very restraints were exciting, making them savor what they could do—the long kisses, the leisurely caressing— while hotly anticipating what came next....the hotel room, where they would be alone and free to immerse themselves in passion, to indulge these urgent incendiary needs.

After a slow ride through the traffic-choked streets, the taxi finally pulled in front of the hotel. Ashlinn and Flint reluctantly drew apart while he paid the cabbie. Their arms draped around each other, the pair raced through the rain, from the curb to the lobby, laughing as the wind blew water around them in swirls.

Inside the hotel, he guided Ashlinn to the elevator, his eyes surveying her possessively. Her lipstick had been erased and her mouth was moist and kiss-swollen, her dark hair tousled. She looked so sexy, as if she'd just climbed out of bed after a hot session of making love.

Which wasn't too far from the actual truth, Flint thought with pure male satisfaction. She had just climbed out of the back seat of a taxi after nearly a half hour of passionate kissing.

And now it was time to do so much more. He held her close to his side as the elevator ascended, wishing it weren't packed with passengers crowded so tightly together that they couldn't even exchange a private word without being overheard.

He settled for smiling down at her. Her eyes met his and she smiled back dreamily, reaching up to squeeze his hand that he'd rested upon her shoulder. It was as if those miserable six weeks of distance and doubt and pain had never occurred, as if they'd made an emotional return back to the lake when they had been so close, so united in body and spirit after making love.

Before everything had suddenly, inexplicably gone wrong.

A shadow crossed his face and Flint leaned down and kissed the top of Ashlinn's head. His usual disdain for public displays of affection seemed to have been entirely dispelled. This time he was not going to let anything come between them.

"The room hasn't been made up yet," Flint observed as he and Ashlinn stepped inside the hotel room.

The bedspread was on the floor, the top sheet and light blanket rumpled at the bottom of the bed, just the way Flint had left it earlier in his rush to go find Camryn.

Camryn! For the first time since seeing Ashlinn in the office, he recalled the original purpose of his trip to New York. He was supposed to bring his wayward little sister back to the university campus in Vermillion.

"Well, it doesn't matter," Ashlinn said.

For a moment Flint was stunned that she'd read his mind and agreed with his decision not to think about the original purpose of this trip. He'd begun to truly doubt that Camryn was in New York anyway. It seemed highly unlikely that he

had arrived at Ashlinn's office by sheer coincidence—more like
sheer scheming by Kaylin and Camryn Paradise instead.

For the first time ever, Flint approved and appreciated their
plotting abilities, no matter what their primary intention might
have been.

Then he realized that Ashlinn wasn't talking about Camryn
at all but about the hotel maids' absence and his unmade bed.

She was already hanging the plastic Do Not Disturb sign on
the knob of the hotel-room door. "We'll only tear the bed up
anyway." She tossed him a sexy glance.

"Tear the bed up?" Flint smirked. "You *are* a lusty wench,
aren't you?"

"Does that scare you? It's not too late to change your mind,
you know." Her tone was solicitously mocking and her dark
eyes dared him. "We could go downstairs to that coffee shop
off the lobby and have lunch, if you'd rather."

"I'm definitely not scared." Flint laughed. "And the only
thing I'm hungry for is you." He closed the door, locking and
chaining it against any possible intruders.

"Let's do it." He caught her hand, tugging her to him.
"Let's tear up that bed."

And they did.

They spent hours in that bed. Kissing, touching, gazing at
each other, admiring what they hadn't been able to see that first
dark night together. Experiencing and sharing pleasures they'd
had neither the time nor the opportunity for during their sole
impetuous tryst in the lake.

The room was filled with the sounds of a man and a woman
making love, the whispers, the moans and sighs, the uncon-
trollable sensual cries of searing and sated passion.

Daylight merged into darkness. Ashlinn and Flint slept and
then woke to more lovemaking, sometimes torrid and urgent,
sometimes languid and voluptuous, the cycle repeated over and
over again.

Neither cared if they were awake or dreaming as their bodies
merged and matched, perfectly attuned in erotic rhythm. There

were only the two of them in this intimate private world, flowing together in a continuous spiral of desire and fulfillment.

It was another need, the prosaic but very pressing demand for food, that finally made Flint switch on the bedside lamp. Ashlinn was lying naked on top of him, her eyes half-closed.

"Almost nine o'clock," he marveled. "No wonder our stomachs are growling. How many meals have we missed, anyway?"

"We're supposed to pretend we didn't hear any stomach growling," Ashlinn corrected lightly, nuzzling his neck. "It's not considered romantic."

"Well, starvation isn't romantic either. Let's call room service and order something fast." Still holding her, Flint reached for the telephone on the nightstand.

"I guess I wouldn't mind a cup of soup and a club sandwich." Just talking about food was making her ravenous. "And a salad and iced tea," she added quickly. "And something for dessert. Pie or cake, nothing chocolate."

"I told you you were hungry." Flint looked pleased, then his expression turned serious. "Ashlinn, we're beyond that initial muddled stage where we have to consider every word and move based on its romantic potential, aren't we?"

They were? Ashlinn gulped, which he interpreted as her assent.

"Good!" His relief was heartfelt. "Romance is phony."

"I guess that's one slogan you won't see embroidered on a decorative throw pillow," she murmured.

"You know what I mean."

"Sure." Ashlinn was glib. "We've moved from the initial muddled stage to the intermediate one."

Would that be the stage which included unexpected pregnancy, along with keeping it a secret? she mused. And then shivered. Discussing romance, phony or not, brought a chilling reality check.

"You're cold." Flint was immediately solicitous and reached for the sheet to pull over them. "I don't want anything muddled between us again, Ashlinn.'' He met her eyes. "The past six weeks was bad enough.''

Between kisses, they'd discussed their mutual misunderstandings. While he was inside her, they had scolded each other for jumping to the wrong conclusions, which they'd agreed had been inordinately stupid ones.

Ashlinn knew that Flint thought there were no more issues between them—and if she weren't pregnant, he would be right. But oddly enough, the one thing they hadn't discussed today had been their lack of protection that night in the lake. The subject hadn't been broached, not even when Flint sheathed himself today, time after time after time. He'd taken meticulous care to be careful today.

Should she have tossed the condoms aside and brightly quipped something about not bothering to lock up the house while the burglar was already inside ransacking?

Probably.

But when Flint was making love to her, her ability to brightly quip deserted her, especially about precautionary measures. Instead, she went soft and weak and thought about love and loving and always being together.

Oh, she'd definitely progressed from an initial muddled stage—to a totally deranged state, Ashlinn decided grimly.

"That lamp is as bright as the big overhead light in TV police shows. The kind they shine in the suspect's face to make him confess,'' she said interrupting her own tortured thoughts and shielding her eyes from the glaring illumination with her hand.

"Do you have something to confess, Miss Carey?'' quizzed Flint, moving his palm up and down her spine in long leisurely strokes.

Ashlinn's breath caught. What an opening! What if she were to say yes, and then just blurt it out? Or perhaps let Flint coax her secret from her?

Should she? *Could* she?

"This is room 534,'' Flint said to the voice on the other end of the line. "And we'd like to order room service.''

Ashlinn went limp as a deflated balloon. She'd missed her chance—not that she had been ready to tell him anyway. Honesty forced her to admit that much to herself. Telling Flint in person was impossible, she decided, as she watched him stride into the bathroom after ordering their food.

Maybe she could tell him the news over the phone when he was back in Sioux Falls; after all, they had desultorily discussed a long-distance relationship earlier this evening.

Ashlinn lay back against the pillows, listening as Flint turned on the water to shower. *Get a grip!* The old catchphrase popped into her head. She'd been notorious in the Carey family for briskly telling others, especially Courtney and Michelle, to "get a grip" when she viewed them as being foolishly overwrought or unrealistic about something. Or someone.

Ashlinn cringed at the memory of her own arrogance.

It was now time to take her own advice. To stop spinning fantasies about Flint and this baby. True, he had made time in his busy schedule to come to New York to straighten things out between them and he'd broached the possibility of keeping in touch from their respective cities.

But that meant he didn't simply consider her a one-night stand as she'd originally thought; it meant he wanted a girlfriend.

What he did not want was a child, not with her or anyone else. As the mother-of-his-child-to-be, there was no place in his life for her.

Get a grip, Ashlinn. She had come to his hotel for one last day with him, and now she'd had that. It was time to face the truth. She was never going to tell Flint about the baby, not in person or over the phone. There would be no long-distance relationship between them either.

It was over.

Eight

"**D**amn it, Ashlinn, open the door!" The shouting was accompanied by an equally ferocious pounding. "I know this is your apartment. I got your address from Carmody."

Inside her apartment, Ashlinn shrank against the bathroom door and tightened the tie of her terry-cloth robe around her. She recognized the voice, of course.

Flint was out in the hall and he was not pleased.

He'd gotten her address? And how had he gotten here so fast? she marveled, even as she trembled in a heightened state of nerves. She had arrived home less than half an hour earlier. Now, just as she was about to get into the shower to wash away all traces of their lovemaking, maybe even to expunge some memories too—Flint was here!

"I know you're there, Ashlinn!" he roared. "Let me in unless you want me to keep this up. And I will, all night if I have to."

Should she risk not opening the door to him? Why not simply take her shower and ignore him? Ashlinn debated. Maybe one of her neighbors would tell him to go away, and when she finally got out of the shower, it would be quiet out in the hall because Flint would be gone.

Her jaw quivered.

"Ashlinn!"

Ashlinn clutched the lapels of her robe tighter. She'd pulled it on the moment she heard Flint out there, unwilling to be naked with him in the vicinity despite the front door with four locks standing between them.

If she were to open that door, she would first have to get dressed and then deal with Flint's indignation at having been left alone in his hotel room. Ashlinn sighed. She wasn't up for all that; better to get into the shower and simply block him out. It might be cowardly, but it was easy, and she had no energy for anything more.

But something happened on her way into the shower. Somehow, she ended up at her front door instead of behind the shower curtain. It was as if she'd been pulled there by some overpowering magnetic force.

"Open this door, Ashlinn!" called Flint.

"You could get arrested if you don't stop that," she warned from her side of the door. "There are stalking laws in this state. I think."

The pounding, the shouting ceased, and the abrupt silence was jarring. And then, "Stalking laws?" Flint repeated incredulously.

She unlocked the top lock. He sounded a bit less angry, and there were three more locks to keep him out, should he revert to fury.

"Do you honestly think I'm stalking you, Ashlinn?"

Had she hurt his feelings? Ashlinn unlocked the next two locks. "No," she admitted. "But my neighbors might, and call the police."

"Let me in, Ashlinn."

At least he'd asked and not demanded. And he wasn't pounding on the door. Ashlinn unlocked the last lock and opened the door a crack.

It was like opening a window when a hurricane was rattling at the pane. Flint flung the door wide open and stormed into her apartment.

Ashlinn gawked at him. He was wearing the trousers of his suit, his shirt was only half buttoned and his belt, tie and coat were conspicuously missing. He didn't resemble the safe, rational businessman who had arrived in the *Tour & Travel* offices this morning. He looked big and strong and primitive—and totally enraged.

She had been fooled by his seemingly calmer demeanor, tricked into opening the door. Ashlinn took several hasty steps backward.

"Will you please explain *this!*" Flint thrust a piece of paper at her while slamming the door shut.

The resounding bang seemed to shake the old apartment building to its foundation.

Ashlinn glanced at the piece of hotel stationery he was holding. "I think it's self-explanatory." She lifted her chin and explained anyway, "It's the note I left when you were in the shower."

Appalled by the threat of veering into melodrama, she had made that note tenaciously upbeat and cheerful. She'd even drawn a smiley face on it to convey goodwill, though cute pictograms weren't her usual style. Her intention had been to make her sudden departure appear uneventful, to avoid making him suspicious of anything.

Instead, she'd made him furious. Ashlinn bit her lip nervously. Now she had no choice but to brazen it out. "Why are you so mad, Flint?" She hoped that she sounded genuinely perplexed.

"The fact that you're even asking is making me madder, Ashlinn."

She managed a weak smile and shrugged, striving to look like someone with nothing to hide. "I don't get it."

"You don't get it?" snarled Flint. He resumed his rampage, except this time he was inside her apartment pacing instead of outside pounding. "I don't get *you,* Ashlinn! Why would you take off like that after we…"

"I explained in the note that I have a lot of work that has to be done tonight," Ashlinn interjected, her own temper rising. At least anger was better than pain or fear. "If you'll remember, I did take the day off to be with you today. Well, everything I needed to do in the office today still has to get finished by tomorrow so I…"

"I don't believe you," Flint cut in sharply. "I saw the chaos you call an office and there is nothing that needs to be done there that can't be postponed—probably indefinitely. So what is the real reason why you ran away from me, Ashlinn?"

"I didn't run away, I went home. And don't you dare judge my staff and—and condemn our office simply because it's different from your anal-retentive Paradise Outdoors headquarters which you enjoy operating as a—a totalitarian regime!"

"Leave Paradise Outdoors out of this. There is no…"

"Uh-oh, I've committed the ultimate crime—mentioning the hallowed Paradise Outdoors in anything less than glowing terms," taunted Ashlinn. "Would lethal injection be sufficent punishment, Mr. Paradise Company Prez?"

He eyed her intently. "Don't try and throw this back on me. I'm not the one at fault here, Ashlinn."

"Fault?" She threw up her hands, then quickly clamped them to her sides. Melodramatic gestures must be avoided, too. "This isn't about assigning blame, it's about me needing to get my work done and you throwing a tantrum because I couldn't stay and have dinner with you. I—I did call and cancel my order from room service so you wouldn't get stuck paying for food that wasn't eaten," she added self-righteously.

"Very considerate of you." Flint was sarcastic. "Too bad you didn't cancel my dinner too. It's probably arrived by now and is sitting outside my hotel-room door."

"You should've stayed and eaten, Flint. You were so hungry." Ashlinn felt chagrined.

"You should've stayed too, Ashlinn. Why didn't you? The real reason, this time."

She ran her hand through her hair, frustration surging through her. "Why won't you believe that I simply have work to do and wanted to get started on it? I was positive that you, of all people, would understand how work takes precedence over anything else. I know that Paradise Outdoors comes first with you, I didn't go ballistic because you have to go back to Sioux Falls tomorrow morning for..."

"Now we're getting somewhere!" exclaimed Flint. "Now you're finally being honest. You're angry because I have to leave tomorrow, so you decided to teach me a lesson by pre-empting me. You decided to leave me first, using work as your excuse. That's petty, Ashlinn."

Petty? Ashlinn stared at him. The behavior he'd described was downright bitchy! Was that how he saw her—as a scheming, temperamental witch? Then it occurred to her that her true reason for running out on him—and that was exactly what she'd done, despite her denial—was infinitely worse.

She had ended their relationship without bothering to tell him it was over, and she'd withheld the reason why as well. Her pregnancy.

Did she have the right to deprive him of that knowledge? Ashlinn's eyes met Flint's, and she was filled with doubt. Her course of action, chosen in his hotel room while he showered, had seemed utterly reasonable at the time. In fact, it had seemed like the best and only thing to do. Now...

Now she wasn't so sure.

"Why did you come over here, Flint?" She was too confused even to try to disguise it.

"Because I didn't want today to end the way it did," he growled. "I thought we'd agreed that the past six weeks were a stupid waste of time. Well, this insipid little note of yours seems designed to insure even more..."

"Insipid? I was being perky," she protested, laughing a little, aware she was perilously close to tears.

"It comes across as less than perky, more like a cheerleader gone berserk." But Flint's anger seemed to be slowly fading. "Ashlinn, I'd like to stay in New York longer, but I really do have an important meeting with one of our major suppliers and..."

"You don't have to explain or apologize, I understand. I—uh—just hope you do, too."

He stared at her for a long silent moment. "Do you mind if I use your phone? I have to make a quick call, one I intended to make at the hotel, but things being how they are..." he shrugged, his voice trailing off.

"Oh sure, go ahead. The phone's right there." She pointed to it, located on the wall just outside her small walk-through kitchen. "If you'd like something to eat, help yourself to anything in the fridge." She pointed to that, too. "I'll—just go take my shower."

She escaped into the bathroom and locked the door, turning on the water before she had time to change her mind. Or before he could follow her in.

Flint glanced at the closed door for a few moments, then reached for the phone. He'd acted on rare impulse tonight—though when he was around Ashlinn, his impulsivity seemed to become commonplace—by rushing over here in a hot-headed fury. But when he had found her gone from his room and seen that note...

Not for a moment had he believed the effusive little note saying that Ashlinn had pressing work to catch up on at home. He still didn't believe it. And her behavior was odd—jumpy and defensive, touchy and almost tearful at times. She seemed more like an edgy stranger, not the woman he'd spent the day with, whom he'd talked and laughed and shared every intimacy with.

Flint listened to the water running in the bathroom. If he hadn't heard the lock click in the door, he might've attempted to walk in on her. There was a very good chance that she wouldn't be able to keep up her guard while naked and wet in his presence.

A hot thrust of arousal ripped through him. He would love to see Ashlinn wet and naked.

But he had heard that lock resolutely turn, and his breaking down Ashlinn's bathroom door would surely not enchant her. Frowning, Flint removed another piece of paper from his pocket and punched in the numbers he'd written down.

"Yeah?" The voice of his half sister Camryn sounded across the line from her dorm room on the USD campus because that was the number he had called.

"Is that the way you always answer the phone?" Flint was momentarily diverted by her atrocious telephone manners.

"Yeah," Camryn replied. "Why?"

"You're not in New York," he said flatly. "Why did Kaylin tell me that you were?"

"She did that?" Camryn laughed. "I wasn't sure if she'd go through with it."

Flint was taken aback by the bold admission. "I thought you would at least make an attempt to deny it." Camryn laughed again. "Will you at least tell me the reason for this—this wild goose chase I was sent on?"

"Did you make up with your lover-girl?"

"What?"

"Well, did you?" Camryn demanded. "That's why Kaylin sent you there. She heard Rafe and Holly talking about how you were moping around after that Ashlinn person went back to New York and…"

"I was *not* moping!" Flint felt himself redden. "I wasn't."

"I don't care either way." Camryn was blunt. "But Kaylin said Rafe mentioned it to Eva who got real freaky. Eva said Ashlinn is just a greedy slut who tried to trap you. You know how jealous Creepy Evita is of her big brothers' attention to anybody but her. She's still burnt by me and Kaylin and Holly living with Rafe, and now this new babe comes along and you…"

"Ashlinn is not a greedy slut, Camryn," Flint said tightly. "Furthermore, I don't believe Eva ever said that she was. That sounds more like *your* brand of insult."

"Eva did too say it," retorted Camryn. "Kaylin and I hope it's true, we hope you really are obsessed with a greedy slut.

But since you didn't seem to be doing anything about it but moping, we figured out a plan to send you to her.''

He felt strangely calm, all things considered, Flint mused, which was not his usual reaction to the girls' schemes. ''Your plan was for Kaylin to pretend she was worried that you'd left school and run away to New York? And that I shouldn't mention anything to Rafe to spare him anxiety?''

''Uh-huh. We thought it was a great way to fix both you and Eva. You take up with the greedy slut again, and Eva flips out because her devoted big brother likes somebody else better than her.'' Camryn's voice rose gleefully. ''Did our plan work? Are you trapped by your New York dream girl?''

''What amuses you more, Camryn? The notion that my dream girl is a greedy slut or that you and Kaylin successfully misled me?''

''Both! But sticking it to Eva is the best part of all!''

''You and Kaylin are very…'' Flint paused.

Words failed him. He knew the younger girls detested Eva; they'd never been shy about expressing their animosity for their half sister. Eva loathed them right back, openly and with equal intensity.

As for him, it seemed that he had been caught in the midst of the ongoing sisterly feud, used as an instrument of revenge by the teens. That he had been led back to Ashlinn, exactly where he wanted to be, only served to make the situation even more bizarre.

It was also ironic that despite their best efforts to sow dissension, Camryn and Kaylin actually had done him a tremendous favor. The joke was on them, he decided, because they had so totally misjudged both Ashlinn and Eva.

''Very conniving,'' he finished mildly. ''And not nearly as clever as you think you are.''

''It would be even better if you moved to New York to be with Dream Girl for good,'' Camryn enthused. ''Eva would be so-o-o ticked off, and we'd be rid of you at the same time!''

''I am *not* moving to New York.''

''I don't recall anyone asking you to,'' replied Ashlinn.

Flint whirled around to see her standing in the doorway. She was wrapped in her white terry robe and had obviously emerged from the bathroom in time to hear him make his declaration to Camryn. The apartment was too small not to be overheard, and he had sounded particularly adamant, mainly to quash his irritating little sister's zeal.

He absently placed the receiver back in its cradle. "I—uh—placed a call to South Dakota. Of course, I used my calling card so you won't be billed for the long-distance charges."

"That's a relief," Ashlinn said snidely. "And now that you've made your call to South Dakota, call yourself a cab to take you back to your hotel."

Flint's lips tightened into a thin straight line. "Do you honestly want me to leave?"

Had Eva really referred to Ashlinn as a greedy slut who had tried to trap him? In spite of his intention to disregard everything Camryn had said, her allegations sneaked insidiously to mind. *Why would Eva make such an accusation?*

She hadn't, he reminded himself. Those devious brats were trying to cause trouble—as usual. Trying to cast Eva in a bad light—as usual.

He folded his arms in front of his chest, his eyes narrowing as he focused on Ashlinn once again. "Well?"

"Yes. I want you to leave, Flint."

Flint stared harder. Her face was flushed and glowing from the humid warmth of the bathroom, moist strands of her dark hair clung to her neck. He knew how soft her skin was, how silky her hair was.

Desire hit him, sharp and fierce. He wanted to touch her face, caress the smooth silk of her body, grasp her hair to hold her head in place while he opened his mouth over hers.

"I'm going to get dressed," announced Ashlinn, and she walked into her bedroom.

Before Flint could decide whether to follow her or not, he heard the damnable click of the door locking again. His decision had been made for him once more. Resentment flooded him.

"You don't have to continually lock your door against me," he called out, incensed. "I'm not going to burst in on you. I happen to be a gentleman, not some slavering, lust-crazed animal," he added indignantly.

Coming here had been a mistake, Flint conceded, scowling. He was tired of trying to interpret Ashlinn. Women could be so difficult to deal with, and Ashlinn Carey had proved to be no exception. Maybe she really did have work to do, maybe she was angry with him for leaving the city tomorrow, maybe she just plain wanted to be alone.

Whatever. He was sick of her treating him like a—a stalker!

Before reaching for the phone to call the taxi, he went into the bathroom, briefly wondering if he should ask her permission first.

No, she probably would tell him to wait till he got back to the hotel, Flint decided testily, and quickly finished.

He was on his way out of the bathroom when a bright blue and white box, on top of a towering pile overflowing the plastic trash can, caught his eye. The words printed on the box seemed to leap into his line of vision. To burn into his consciousness.

Pregnancy Test.

Nothing could have prevented him from picking up that box. From reading every word on it.

He heard a small gasp and looked up to see Ashlinn standing a few feet away, wearing old ripped jeans and a faded Yankees baseball shirt. If she had deliberately chosen her attire to dim her allure, she needn't have bothered. Sex was the last thing on his mind at this particular moment.

"The stick with the test result isn't in the box," Flint said quietly. "Where is it, Ashlinn?"

Ashlinn blanched. Her eyes looked like huge dark saucers. "In the trash somewhere," she mumbled.

They both glanced at the overstuffed trash can.

"Am I going to have to search the trash for it, or are you going to tell me the results, Ashlinn?"

For a split second, Ashlinn feared she might faint. But the moment passed, and all her fighting instincts rushed to the fore.

Even as a child, she'd never been the weepy shrinking type; when cornered, she had always been one who fought back. She was cornered now.

"What makes you think it has anything to do with you, anyway?" She made herself meet his steely-eyed gaze.

Flint muttered a curse and overturned the trash can, spilling the contents all over the floor. The pregnancy test box lay amidst tissues, gum wrappers, cotton balls, a squeezed-flat tube of toothpaste, burnt matchsticks.... He spotted the plastic stick and snatched it up.

"Congratulations. According to this, you're going to be a mother."

"I know." She held her head higher.

Her defiance rocked him. Weren't pregnant women supposed to be hyperemotional, subject to bursting into tears at any given moment? Ashlinn looked more ready to take a swing at him instead.

"Are you going to admit that it happened six weeks ago in the lake, or do we have to go through DNA testing after the baby is born?" His eyes seemed to bore into her. "Assuming that it is born. Have you made a decision about that?"

"Is this where you offer me money to get rid of it?" It hurt to say the words.

Hearing them caused Flint to flinch. "What did I do to deserve that, Ashlinn?"

"You mean, aside from having unprotected sex with me in that lake and then not bothering to call me for six weeks? Not mentioning the possibility of—of any consequences? You never did, not that night or for the next six weeks. And you didn't say a word about it today either. You were careful not to ask, and I got your message loud and clear. Don't ask, don't tell. So I didn't."

The words, the pain and anger, seemed to pour out of her, and she couldn't stop. Aghast, Ashlinn listened to herself as if caught in somebody else's bad dream. Suddenly, she was crying. Tears poured down her cheeks and her body shook with sobs as hysteria rose within her. She could feel herself sliding out of control. It was scary yet exhilarating at the same time, like being in the front car of a roller coaster plunging down a dark steep drop.

"You never answered my question," persisted Flint. "Are you going to have it?"

"Oh, what do you care, anyway?" She began to pick up the trash on the floor and throw it back into the can, pausing to grab fresh tissues to wipe her streaming eyes.

Flint stood still, watching her. "Yes or no, Ashlinn? I have a right to know."

She didn't answer; she just kept crying and picking up the scattered trash. Finally, losing patience, Flint gripped her arms and pulled her upright, holding her in front of him.

"You've kept this a secret long enough, Ashlinn. Tell me!"

"Suppose I say, yes, I'm going to keep the baby." She tried to wriggle out of his grasp, to no avail. His hands were as strong and unyielding as steel clamps. "What then, Flint?"

"Then I think we should get married immediately," Flint said without missing a beat.

"Married?" Ashlinn nearly choked on the word. She envied his aplomb. How did he manage it? But at least his proposal, or whatever it was, had one positive effect. The shock of it abruptly, immediately, stopped her tears. "You can't be serious!"

"Well, I am." He dropped his hands and moved away from her, halfway across the room.

His need to put distance between them struck Ashlinn as symbolic of his true feelings. "You don't want to get married," she cried, and waited for him to comment.

He said nothing.

"Besides, we hardly know each other," she prompted.

Which did draw a response from him. "That falls into the category of water over the dam, as my father used to say."

"As long as we're quoting fathers, here's one from my dad—'Marry in haste, repent at leisure.' This isn't the shotgun-wedding era, Flint. In case you haven't noticed, lots of people

who aren't married have babies these days. Just look at all the
magazine covers featuring…''

''I don't ascribe to the 'everybody's doing it' school of
thought,'' Flint interrupted. ''I never have, not in business, not
in anything, especially this. If I have a kid, I'm damn well
going to know where it is and how it is, and that means it's
going to live with me.''

''What about me?'' Ashlinn shot back. ''It's mine too, you
know. I'm the mother.''

''Which is why we're getting married. We'll all live together, the three of us. I spent too many years watching my
father mourn his long-lost kids, wondering where they were,
what they were doing, whether they were safe and healthy or
miserable. It was torture for him and I am not—I repeat—*I am
not* going to live through that myself, Ashlinn.''

She was startled by his vehemence. She'd been expecting
him to—what? To be indifferent? She wasn't sure, but she
hadn't thought he would try to lay claim to his child.

''I wouldn't just drop out of sight with the baby, Flint. A
life on the run strikes me as something straight out of *Days of
Our Lives*.''

''You'd relegate me to occasional visitation rights and phone
calls from New York instead? No, Ashlinn.'' His voice was
firm and decisive. ''Hand in your resignation tomorrow and
arrange for a moving company to have your things sent to
Sioux Falls. I'll have my secretary Nancy make reservations
for you on a flight out at the end of the week.''

''You sound like you're issuing orders to your lackeys at
Paradise Outdoors! Well, I'm not one of them.''

''I do not employ lackeys. Let's keep this personal and leave
Paradise Outdoors out of it, Ashlinn.''

''We can't leave *Tour & Travel* out of it. What about the
magazine? I can't just quit my job, I'm the only one there who
knows how to put an issue together. Mr. Oakes is depending
on me.''

''Give me a sizable break, Ashlinn.'' Flint laughed scorn-
fully. ''You made your opinion of your boss unmistakably

clear during the first five minutes that we met, so don't bother to pretend that you feel any sense of duty or loyalty to him.''

"I'm talking about Mr. Oakes Sr., Junior's father. *He* gave me a raise and put me temporarily in charge of *Tour & Travel.*''

"You mean you're the boss now?" Flint was astonished.

"Yes!" Ashlinn bristled. "Do you have to look so utterly amazed? Why shouldn't I be in charge? I've been there longer than anyone else on the staff, I have a degree in English and I…''

"…have no control whatsoever over the wild bunch in that office," Flint put in. "Of course, they appeared to be a recalcitrant lot who wouldn't listen to anybody," he added quickly.

"You don't have to patronize me," snapped Ashlinn. "I know you're thinking that *you* could have them working at one hundred percent productivity if given a chance."

"Stop putting words in my mouth and listen to the ones I'm actually speaking. I saw those slackers goofing off today, and I'm willing to bet that nothing gets done around there. Since you can't put out the magazine single-handedly and Oakes Sr. is no dope, it won't take him long to decide *Tour & Travel* is a lost cause and shut it down."

"So I should consider your gracious offer to be a good career move? I should marry you and move to Sioux Falls because *Tour & Travel* is about to go under?"

Flint heaved a sigh. "All right, Ashlinn, if that's the way you want to look at it, yes. You're single, pregnant and about to be out of work. Yes, marrying me is definitely in your best interests, Ashlinn."

"How could I possibly resist such a romantic proposal?" Ashlinn's fingers idly brushed the hardcover world atlas lying on an end table. "Yet somehow, I can. You can take your offer of marriage and…''

"Don't even think of throwing that, Ashlinn," Flint warned. Menace suddenly glittered in his eyes as he stared at the atlas. "We might as well begin by setting a few ground rules, and the first one is no flying books, plates, lamps or anything else."

"I wasn't going to throw anything at you," retorted Ashlinn. "I hardly realized I was touching..." She broke off, curiosity overcoming her irritation. "Is that how you grew up? With barbarians throwing stuff at each other?"

"Never my mother and father," Flint said stiffly. "But during his marriage to Marcine, Dad was always getting hit by something she'd thrown. Rafe and Eva and I sometimes got caught in the crossfire, too. One time, poor little Eva was clipped by the corner of a cookbook that cut her just above her eyebrow. She had to get four stitches and still has a small scar, a battle scar from one of South Dakota's worst marriages."

"Marcine sounds like a real gem." Ashlinn grimaced. "And you think I'm a book-throwing maniac just like her? Thanks a lot."

She sank onto the plaid slip-covered sofa and rested her head wearily on her hands. "If you're so ready to think the worst of me, why bother with marriage, even a short marriage of convenience? And don't say it's for the baby's sake because you don't care about the baby. You don't want it, you've never wanted children, and..."

"Who said I never wanted children?" he cut in hotly.

"You did, in my office earlier. You said children were a catastrophe, and..."

"I didn't—what I meant was—I didn't mean that." He shook his head in frustration. "You completely misinterpreted me, Ashlinn. Let me set the record straight. I don't think our child is a catastrophe."

She wanted to believe him. Ashlinn gulped back a sob of despair. Wanting to believe, no matter what? She was truly hooked.

"You don't have a very high opinion of me, Ashlinn." Flint was grim. "You think I hate children, even my own. You even accused me of deliberately ignoring the possibility that you might be pregnant."

Ashlinn rallied a little. "Which you did, didn't you?"

"No. I actually thought of it that night at the lake, but you were so damn unapproachable afterward that I..." He shook his head. "There's no point in rehashing all that again. I thought we'd already sorted out our misunderstandings this afternoon. What I thought. What you thought. Well, we were both wrong about what the other thought, weren't we?"

"It doesn't matter, Flint. I don't care."

"It does matter and you sure as hell do care." He sat down beside her. "And I'm offering reasons, not excuses. I didn't simply forget our—lapse, Ashlinn. I even asked Eva about..."

"You told your sister about us?" Ashlinn bolted to her feet. "How could you?"

He caught her hands and yanked her off-balance, tumbling her onto his lap. "Calm down, Ashlinn. I didn't mention you by name, I was speaking hypothetically to Eva. She told me that sophisticated women take sexual responsibility for themselves," he quoted his sister. "So, rightly or not, I suppose I concluded..."

"...that I'm either naive or conniving or totally irresponsible?" Ashlinn was so outraged she forgot to fight her way off his lap. She stayed put, glaring at him. "I guess that completely lets you off the hook, doesn't it, Flint? It's all my fault since I'm *sophisticated.* Oh, and I know exactly what your sister Eva means by that, too. For 'sophisticated'—substitute 'easy lay.'"

Sophisticated women take sexual responsibility for themselves. The words and the implication behind them burned her.

"Look, I'm sorry I ever mentioned it," Flint said impatiently. "What happened, happened and we're getting married. End of story."

"It's the end, all right. But we aren't getting married." She was suddenly acutely aware that she was sitting on his lap, and she tried to pull away, to get to her feet.

Flint held her firmly in place—probably because she wanted to get up, not because he wanted her there, Ashlinn decided darkly. She didn't want to be so close to him, not under these circumstances. She remembered how it had been earlier today in his hotel room when she'd been on his lap, nude and intimately joined with him, so in love with him.

Ashlinn swallowed hard. She was still in love with him, but

whatever he'd felt for her before had been displaced by his grim, unremitting sense of duty, of that she was certain. And as far as she was concerned, duty ranked right up there with pity as a prime killer of blossoming love.

"Let me go!" She struggled to be free. "Your fingers are practically imprinted into my skin. You're hurting me," she added for extra effect—even though he wasn't.

A thrill spun through her when he immediately removed his hands from her, releasing her. He'd been conscientious about her level of comfort during the camping trip; he'd exhibited the same concern for her today in the hotel. Knowing he was still that way, even now, when he undoubtedly hated her guts, was oddly reassuring.

She quickly scrambled off his lap. He stood up and they faced each other like two wary adversaries—who were having a baby!

"I'm postponing my trip home," Flint stated after the silence stretched on, too long and fraught with tension. "My staff can…"

"…survive without you? Impossible, Flint," she taunted. "The company will go under without your fundamental presence."

Flint didn't rise to the bait. "My staff is quite capable and will manage effectively without me for a while. I want to help you make moving arrangements and wrap up loose ends here," he said with a calm that chilled her. "Then I'll fly back to Sioux Falls with you."

"Wrap up loose ends? You're talking about my life, Flint!" Her heart was pounding so hard and so fast she wouldn't have been surprised if it had burst out of her chest. "I can't just leave…"

"You can and you will."

"What about your important meeting tomorrow with one of your major suppliers?" she tried desperately. "It's too crucial for you to miss, isn't it?"

"Like you care." A ghost of a smile flitted across his face. "You're really grasping at straws with that one, Ashlinn." He walked to the front door, opening it to let himself out. "I'll see you tomorrow morning. Would you prefer I come here or to the *Tour & Travel* office?"

"I'll be at the office, as usual," she said in her most imperious tone. "Preferably, you'll be back in Sioux Falls."

"When I go back to Sioux Falls, you'll be with me—as Mrs. Paradise."

As an exit line, it was superb. By the time Ashlinn recovered her wits to marshal a comeback, he was gone. She stared at the door he'd closed behind him.

Mrs. Paradise! Emotion surged through her, fierce and physical. She felt like crying—or maybe throwing up.

She ended up doing neither. As if in a daze, she trooped over to the door and locked all four locks. Suddenly she was exhausted. She knew she should begin working on some sort of escape plan; after all, she didn't have too many hours left until tomorrow morning when Flint would attempt to take control of her life.

But she was just too tired to do anything but drag herself into her bedroom, change into her favorite pajamas, big boxy-style cotton PJs with cows and clouds printed on a sky-blue background. If Flint's tastes in women's sleepwear included sexy negligees or cut-out baby-doll nighties, he was in for a big disappointment when he saw hers.

Musing on that satisfying bit of vengeance, Ashlinn fell asleep.

Nine

"**A**shlinn, I can't believe you're getting married." Courtney Carey Tremaine's big dark eyes, so similar to her sister's, shone with excitement. "You've kept everything such a secret, especially Flint! You didn't even let anybody know you were dating anyone special. But you've always had a secretive side," she added, half-admiring, half-accusing.

"She's always valued her privacy and probably didn't want to risk jinxing things with Flint by talking about him, right, Ashlinn?" suggested Michelle Carey Saraceni, who was eager to give Ashlinn the benefit of the doubt.

Ashlinn nodded absently, watching two-year-old Sarah Tremaine circle the small round table where the tiered wedding cake sat. Sarah's father, Connor, stood close by in case intervention was required, while cradling three-month-old Nina in the crook of one arm.

Ashlinn debated whether to distract Connor—maybe she could swipe the dozing baby's pacifier, thus waking her—to give Sarah a crack at the cake. The little girl moved with lightning speed and could dismantle anything in record time. An attack on that cake would be a perfect diversionary tactic, providing Ashlinn with one last chance to escape this farce...

"We all like Flint, Ashlinn," continued Courtney. "He's nice and he's cute and..."

"Puppies are cute, Courtney," said Steve Saraceni, joining them while bouncing his year-old daughter, Julie, in his arms. "Babies are cute. Flint Paradise is all male, a man's man, no resemblance to the assortment of pinheads and dorks we've seen Ashlinn bossing around in years past. But hey, Flint wants to marry her, so let's get the ceremony over before he changes his mind."

"Steve is just joking, Ashlinn," Michelle quickly assured her. "You know that, don't you?" She moved fast to intercept Jake, Julie's twin, before the exuberant toddler could race out of the private hotel dining room that had been reserved for the small post-wedding reception.

The tables were set, flowers were in place and Ashlinn and her various family members were waiting for Flint to arrive with the retired judge he'd found to perform the civil ceremony.

"Sure. Steve is such a joker," murmured Ashlinn, realizing full well that brother-in-law Steve was needling her with all the gusto of a full-fledged sibling.

Possibly she deserved it, she conceded. After all, she'd been excessively negative and uncooperative when Steve had been dating Michelle because she thought he was a too-smooth operator who would hurt her innocent, too-trusting stepsister.

Steve had not forgotten Ashlinn's hostility, and it was definitely payback time for him. Last night upon meeting Flint for the first time, Steve had gleefully presented Ashlinn's husband-to-be with a copy of *Hooked!*

Last night, all of them—Courtney and Connor, Michelle and Steve, Flint and Ashlinn and the four small children—had been in Flint's hotel suite for a brief prenuptial reunion.

It had been Flint who'd put it together, who had called the Tremaines and the Saracenis and invited them to New York

for the wedding. He'd also called the other Carey extended
family members—her parents, Warren, Hayden, Cathy and
Mark—to invite them and their families to the wedding as well.
Only Courtney and Michelle, in nearby Washington and Harrisburg, had been able to attend on such short notice, with their
husbands and children in tow.

"Just thought you might like a little peek into your bride's
psyche, Flint," Steve had declared with jovial charm. "According to Ashlinn's book, men get women sexually addicted
to them and then treat them badly, and the poor women can't
do anything about it because they're *hooked!*" He chuckled
genially, inviting everybody else to enjoy the joke with him.

Steve was skillfully charming, which initially had raised a
red flag with Ashlinn. She equated easy charm with insincerity,
which was probably why she had fallen so fast for Flint Paradise, she mused moodily. Flint had been prickly, even surly,
when they'd first met. Certainly no one could accuse him of
bowling her over with his scintillating charm.

"Sex is the lure and the trap that keeps women helplessly
snared in relationships that aren't good for them?" Flint read
the back-cover blurb.

"Nothing like some good old purple prose, huh?" Steve
laughed. "And that book is full of it."

Ashlinn scowled at him. "Okay, maybe I shouldn't have
tried to convince Michelle that she'd been 'hooked!' by you,
Steve, but passing around that professional embarrassment of
a book is a low blow. I thought I'd confiscated and destroyed
all the remaining family copies." She made a grab for the book
in Flint's hands.

Flint didn't relinquish it. "I'd like to read your book, Ashlinn."

"Why? I already told you it was a flop," growled Ashlinn,
shooting Steve another baleful look.

"It was interesting," Michelle said loyally. "It should have
been a bestseller."

"Not in today's market. *Hooked!* is about pathetic women

who love the wrong men too much, and nobody wants to read about them anymore," explained Courtney, who followed trends in entertainment.

"You mean, somebody wanted to read about them in the first place?" quizzed Flint, incredulous.

"The market shifts." Courtney shrugged. "Empowered women are what's hot these days, women who don't rely on men to make them happy, who can fend for themselves and do it well, who *insist* on doing so. Just look at the current TV shows with all those self-reliant, kick-butt heroines, the vampire-slayers and witches and no-nonsense detectives. Look at today's music with all the women singer-songwriters telling men they're not willing to be anybody's doormat."

"Courtney, I think you just described Ashlinn herself," declared Michelle.

"Why don't you write a new book about strong, empowered women, Ashlinn?" suggested Connor. "You could do that."

He and Ashlinn had buried the hatchet at little Sarah's first birthday party last year. When Ashlinn apologized for considering him a snake, Connor offered his own apology for believing she was cold as an iceberg.

"How about writing one about witches, Ashlinn?" Steve grinned. "There's a subject you could do a lot with."

"Ashlinn can write another book about whatever she wants when we're back home in Sioux Falls," Flint said, still leafing through *Hooked!* "She'll have plenty of time and opportunity."

"I'm so happy you're getting married, but I'm sad you'll be moving so far away, Ashlinn." Michelle looked distressed. She turned to Flint. "We see each other just about every other month, but when you're in South Dakota..."

"We have flights between Sioux Falls and Harrisburg," Flint consoled her. "Although I can't promise regular bi-monthly visits."

"Don't worry, we'll all adjust," Steve was quick to offer reassurance.

"Do you think you'll get back to New York, Ashlinn?"

asked Courtney. "I know how much you've loved living here."

"Yes." Ashlinn's eyes misted.

She still couldn't believe she was leaving the city; it seemed unreal. But the events leading up to her departure were very real indeed.

The moving company hired by Flint had arrived yesterday and packed up the contents of her apartment. And in what she had considered a shockingly high-handed move, Flint had written and faxed her resignation from the magazine to Presley Oakes Sr. because the mogul was currently in Australia.

She had argued, she had railed over every step, but Flint was relentless. He was a high-energy CEO used to taking charge, and during his five-day sojourn in New York he had directed every ounce of his drive to orchestrating Ashlinn's move to Sioux Falls—as Mrs. Flint Paradise.

She had never actually agreed to marry him, Ashlinn reminded him furiously after he'd sent the job-ending fax. Yet she knew in her heart of hearts she wanted nothing more, which was why she hadn't sabotaged the fax's transmittal.

Flint remained undaunted. "You know you're going to, Ashlinn. It's just a matter of when," he had replied with a confidence bordering on arrogance. "So why not now? The sooner the better, I say."

"You're so sure of yourself!" She hurled the words at him. "But you have no reason to be so sure of me, Flint."

"Yes I do, Ashlinn. You don't want to raise a child alone, you know how difficult it would be, both for you and the kid. And most of all, you don't want to tell your folks that you're pregnant and unmarried. That's my trump card."

And it was. For although she hadn't voiced it, Flint had correctly divined one of her major dreads. Tell Mom and Dad, who were happily retired in Florida and proud of their adult offspring, that she was pregnant without a husband in sight?

It was unimaginable. The senior Careys embodied family values before it became a catchphrase and would be devastated by what she knew they would call her "plight."

Ashlinn didn't want to disappoint them; she didn't want to be worried over, or to have a plight. And Flint knew it, the snake! He knew it and used it to pursue his objectives.

Since he had learned she was carrying his child, he'd been in overdrive, making arrangements for their marriage and her move to Sioux Falls while she had lapsed into an uncharacteristic passivity, offering admittedly weak protests but nothing else.

There had been only one area in which she had prevailed, and that was sex. She had refused to make love with him, offering a plethora of excuses. That she was exhausted, that she felt sick, that she wanted to wait until they were married. Ashlinn was vaguely aware that control and the loss of it figured in her refusal to experience sexual pleasure with Flint. She was surrendering everything to him, her independence, her freedom, even her name. She wouldn't surrender her body and her self-control to him too.

But they didn't discuss her reasons and refusals. Flint accepted them all and never pressed her, leaving her each night with an almost chaste goodnight kiss.

And he kept making plans, setting things in motion. Which brought them to this point, five days after Flint's arrival in New York.

Their wedding day...

For her wedding, Ashlinn wore an elegant blue silk dress that Flint had insisted on buying for her. He had also ordered her a wedding bouquet of white roses.

She stood with Courtney, trying to fend off her sister's increasingly suspicious questions.

Michelle rejoined them, having deposited little Jake with his father. Now Steve held both twins who wriggled and giggled in his arms.

"I know something's going on," pressed Courtney. "I thought it was strange that Flint was the one to call and invite us, but he seems so nice and normal that I let myself be lulled into thinking everything is all right. But it's not, is it?"

Ashlinn debated telling Courtney that nothing was right, that she was pregnant and Flint was pushing her into a marriage that she didn't want.

Except she didn't want the alternative either, Ashlinn admitted to herself. She didn't want Flint to return to South Dakota alone while she stayed in New York, unmarried, pregnant...and unemployed. Courtney would offer financial aid, of that Ashlinn had no doubt. So would Michelle and the others. But she didn't want to have to depend on family charity, either.

Had she ever been so conflicted, wanting, not wanting, uncertain and unsure?

"I'm—just nervous about moving," said Ashlinn. At least that wasn't a complete lie. "All that moving we did as kids when Dad was transferred from one army post to another made me want to stay put as an adult."

"I know what you mean," Michelle said, her voice warm with empathy. "I felt the same way about putting down roots in one place. And you will, Ashlinn—in Sioux Falls with Flint. He's crazy about you, I can tell."

Ashlinn winced. "You're such a starry-eyed romantic, Michelle."

"Shouldn't you be starry-eyed and romantic today too, Ashlinn?" Courtney eyed her sharply. "After all, it's your wedding day, which is usually considered a day for such things."

What she was actually feeling was as far from romantic and starry-eyed as one could get, Ashlinn decided grimly. Unabashed terror was closer to the mark; she was giving up everything in her life that was familiar to her. Her wild dark eyes met Michelle's serene blue eyes.

"Don't worry, Ashlinn, I was scared on my wedding day, too," soothed Michelle. "Dad and my mom and your mom all said it's perfectly normal."

"There's Flint," exclaimed Courtney. "And he's with..." Her jaw dropped. "He's with his double! You didn't tell us that Flint had an identical twin, Ashlinn."

"She didn't tell us about Flint," Michelle pointed out. "So it's kind of natural she didn't mention his twin, either."

Ashlinn watched Flint stride purposefully into the room accompanied by an older man in a black robe, obviously the judge, and a much younger man with an expensive camera— a photographer?—and Rafe Paradise.

Courtney was right. Rafe really was Flint's double.

Ashlinn stared at the twin brothers and, for an awful moment, wondered which was which. Then she recognized the tie she and Flint had bought earlier in the week. With that identifying marker in place, she began to spot the slight differences between the pair.

Flint's hair was a bit shorter and he wore his watch on his right arm since he was left-handed. She knew what side his hair was parted on, and in mirror image, Rafe's was parted on the opposite side.

The brothers' eyes, dark and wide set, slightly almond shaped and arched by black brows, were identical upon first glance, but Flint's gaze was piercing and intense while Rafe appeared relaxed and a bit curious.

Flint's expression as he walked toward her was frankly possessive and sexual. Ashlinn felt a small shiver tingle along her spine as their eyes met. No other man had ever looked at her in that particular way. While she was trying to decide if that was a good or a bad thing, Flint reached her side.

"Sorry, we're a little late." He slipped his arm around her waist and leaned down to kiss her cheek. "This is Judge McKown and George Granger, the photographer, and of course, my…"

"It's good to see you again, Ashlinn." Rafe Paradise came to stand on her other side and gave her a hearty fraternal hug, as if he actually remembered who she was, as if he wasn't flabbergasted that this total stranger was marrying his twin. "I've already congratulated Flint on his good taste. He's a very lucky guy."

"Thank you, Rafe."

Ashlinn was grateful for the charade. Without supplying any details, she and Flint had led her family to believe that their relationship was of a much longer duration than it really was.

By acting as if he knew her well and was unsurprised by this wedding, Rafe's performance supported their little secret.

She wondered if Flint had told his brother about the baby, or if Rafe had already guessed. Whatever her sisters' suspicions about this quickie wedding, they tactfully had not voiced them.

Introductions were made all around.

"I'm glad you could come, Rafe," Ashlinn said quietly, and realized that she really was. Flint should have his twin at his side when he got married. "I was afraid you might not be able to come on such short notice."

"And miss being my brother's best man?" Rafe smiled. "Never! Although you two don't believe in long engagements, do you?"

"Don't go there, Rafe," said Flint, and everybody laughed.

Only Ashlinn knew that he definitely wasn't kidding.

"Who is the maid of honor?" asked the photographer. "I'd like to get a picture of the bride and groom and their attendants."

"That would be *matron* of honor," corrected Steve. "No matter who it is."

Ashlinn looked at Michelle and Courtney, who'd stood up for each other at their own respective weddings. "I haven't even thought about choosing a maid—matron of honor."

"I know that none of us are surprised to hear that." Courtney sighed.

"Why don't I flip a coin?" suggested Flint. He dug a quarter out of his pocket. "Call it, Michelle."

"Tails," exclaimed Michelle.

"Tails, it is," announced Flint, glancing at the coin he'd flipped. He didn't offer to show it, but immediately shoved it back into his pocket.

Ashlinn caught his eye and he grinned. Note to self, she thought, ask Flint if it really was tails, or if he had guessed she wanted to choose Michelle, to whom she had always been closer.

"Shall we get started?" suggested the judge.

For a life-altering event, the wedding was remarkably short.

After Flint and Ashlinn said their vows and exchanged rings, Judge McKown pronounced them husband and wife by the powers vested in him by the state of New York. He gave Flint permission to kiss the bride and Flint lightly brushed her mouth with his. Ashlinn's eyes dropped shut and her lips parted. The swift caress whetted her sensual appetite for her new husband.

George Granger prowled the room, snapping pictures of everybody.

The judge declined an invitation to join the group for lunch and left. Everybody took their seats, and lunch was served.

Predictably, all four children began to fuss as soon as the food arrived.

"Luckily there are four parents here, so each baby gets an adult of its own," observed Rafe with a smile, watching the interaction.

Ashlinn, seated between the twin brothers, looked from one to the other, wondering once again how much Flint had told Rafe.

"Our sisters and my wife are really sorry they couldn't make it for the wedding, Ashlinn," Rafe said gamely, in another attempt at conversation. "But they're looking forward to getting together with you and Flint in Sioux Falls as soon as possible."

Ashlinn simply couldn't envision it, she and Flint as a married couple "getting together in Sioux Falls" with the rest of the Paradise clan. Or with anyone else there, for that matter.

She glanced down at the unfamiliar sight of the gold wedding band on her finger. Flint wore an identical one; he'd purchased them both at a jewelry store the same day they had shopped for his tie and her wedding dress.

Ashlinn had refused to go with him into the jewelry store, heading into a bookstore instead. She'd still been in denial, unable to believe that this marriage was truly going to happen. Buying rings made it too real, and so she had avoided it. Even their blood tests and trip to city hall for the marriage license didn't drive home the inexorable reality of what was to come.

But it had really happened. Here she sat with the new wedding ring on her finger, a plate of chicken-something in front of her, Flint's wife, after all.

She guessed that Rafe probably considered her socially inept because she didn't reply to either of his comments, but at this point, she felt incapable of chatting casually with anyone. She laid down her fork, unable to eat, either.

Flint noticed. Though his attention appeared to be focused solely on his plate, Ashlinn realized he was actually avoiding glancing to his left, where Courtney sat openly breast-feeding baby Nina. He kept his discomfiture concealed, but Ashlinn was aware of it. She was surprised how well she recognized his subtle signs of unease.

And he seemed to know hers as well. "Aren't you feeling well, Ashlinn?" he asked, his voice husky with concern.

Ashlinn blushed and shot him a quelling glance. Questions like that would only alert everybody to—her condition.

"I'm fine." She picked up her fork and determinedly speared a piece of chicken.

"Better eat hearty," advised Rafe. "Otherwise, you'll be doomed to airport cuisine. We have an ungodly travel day ahead of us today, don't we? Flying back to Sioux Falls via Atlanta, going south and east to get north and west. We won't arrive till late tonight. Too bad we couldn't get a direct flight."

"Believe me, I tried," said Flint. "But there aren't any."

"T-today?" stammered Ashlinn. "We're leaving today?"

This time Rafe put down his fork and looked uneasy. "I—uh—thought you knew."

"Flint!" Ashlinn turned to face him so quickly, her long dark hair flew out around her shoulders, the ends whipping at Rafe. "You didn't say we were leaving today!"

Her voice was thick with panic. It was too much, the arrival of her family yesterday, keeping up the pretense around them that everything was normal when it was anything but. And then today, this wedding. This marriage.

"You didn't ask," Flint said simply.

"I won't…" She paused and had to gulp for air because

she'd forgotten to breathe and felt as if she were suffocating. "I'm not leaving today, Flint. I—you—"

"We're leaving for the airport right after lunch, Ashlinn," Flint replied in his executive voice, the one that ruled Paradise Outdoors.

He'd been ruling her these last five days, Ashlinn acknowledged rebelliously. And she'd let him. Well, not anymore! "No, I'm not going to go."

"Ashlinn, it's not up for discussion."

"You're right, we're not discussing anything. You're issuing orders—and I'm *not* following them."

"Flint, you really can't blame her for being upset." To Ashlinn's surprise, Rafe came to her defense. "For crying out loud, it's your wedding day. And your wedding night. It's one thing if she'd agreed to spend it on planes and in airports between flights, but for her not to know…"

Rafe shook his head, his tone, his expression conveying his belief that Flint had blundered spectacularly. "She's a new bride, Flint. She was probably expecting to spend a leisurely afternoon with you, to have a romantic dinner and then—well, a nice wedding night in a classy hotel. Am I right, Ashlinn?"

"Tell him just how wrong he is, Ashlinn," Flint said wryly.

There was really no choice between Rafe, who was regarding her sympathetically, or Flint, determined to have things his way.

"Rafe is right. I had my heart set on dinner at the Rainbow Room. And—and a carriage ride in Central Park. I hoped you'd made reservations to spend tonight in a suite at the Plaza, Flint. I kept dropping so many hints, I was sure you'd picked up on them."

She was lying through her teeth and anyone who knew her well would know it. A carriage ride in Central Park? Her? But Rafe Paradise listened to her with growing alarm, and she knew he was buying every word.

"Ohhh, Flint." Rafe rested his arms on the table and clutched his head with his hands. "You blew it, brother."

Flint actually laughed. "The Rainbow Room, huh? A carriage ride and a night at the Plaza. Points to you for creativity under the gun, Ashlinn. Next time we're in New York, we'll do all those things. Especially the carriage ride, I promise.''

Rafe looked worried. ''Flint, can I offer you a little advice? Don't always insist on having the upper hand. One thing I've learned from being married is how to compromise—and to communicate,'' he added earnestly.

''You're starting to sound like one of those feel-good gurus, Rafe,'' Flint admonished lightly. ''Guess that goes with the territory when you're married to a shrink.''

''Time to toast the bride and groom!'' Connor stood up to make the announcement.

Ashlinn and Flint's argument was put on hold as Rafe offered the toast to the happy couple, with Dom Perignon champagne supplied by Courtney and Connor.

Ashlinn hardly heard a word of Rafe's heartfelt toast. She was staring at the glass of champagne bubbling in the goblet in front of her. Alcohol was not recommended during pregnancy, but would a few sips of champagne hurt?

George Granger was ready to take the traditional shot of the bride and groom drinking the traditional toast. Following the photographer's instructions, Ashlinn linked her arm with Flint's and lifted the glass. It would be noticeable if she didn't imbibe, especially such an expensive brand as Dom Perignon. Her family knew she wasn't a teetotaler. She might as well announce her pregnancy here and now, confirming what they undoubtedly expected, if she didn't drink the champagne.

Her eyes met Flint's.

''Don't worry,'' he murmured softly. It helped that baby Nina and Michelle's twins were all howling in unison, drowning him out. ''I'll take care of it.''

He bumped her hand, spilling her champagne with such deft precision, it looked like a genuine accident. The contents of her glass splashed down the front of her blue silk dress.

''I'm sorry, sweetheart,'' Flint exclaimed with credible remorse. ''I'm so clumsy! Now you're all wet and will have to change. What a shame, that dress is so beautiful on you, too.''

Ashlinn began to laugh as tears simultaneously filled her eyes. Flint had not only known she was anxious about the toast, he also knew why, and had taken action to allow her to keep her secret a bit longer.

Before they sat back down, he traced his thumb along the curve of her jaw. "Just keep in mind that I'm on your side, Ashlinn."

She was going to cry if she didn't pull herself together. Characteristically, Ashlinn rallied.

"I have to admire how subtly you worked in that crack about my dress," she said glibly, leaning in close to him so only he could hear.

"I thought you'd appreciate it." He caught her hand and carried it to his mouth, pressing his lips to her palm. "Why don't you go change now? It can't be comfortable to be doused in champagne."

"It isn't. I think I will." Ashlinn slipped out of her seat and headed for the door. "Go ahead and have the cake, everybody," she called over her shoulder to their guests. "I'll be back soon."

She was grateful for the reprieve. It was absolutely necessary, and not because of her damp dress. The sensation of Flint's mouth against her palm had sent prickles of electricity straight to her core, underscoring her susceptibility to his touch. Denying him access to her body all week long seemed to have backfired on her. Instead of weaning her away from desiring him, her need had only been enhanced.

Ashlinn took the elevator to the third floor where Flint had booked her a room last night after her furniture's departure for Sioux Falls. She had three suitcases packed to tide her over until all her belongings arrived in South Dakota, and Ashlinn quickly delved into one to pull out a pair of black leggings and a long sapphire-blue cotton sweater.

It was a relief to shed her dress and her panty hose which contained just enough spandex to make them uncomfortably tight. She felt free and unrestrained in her black panties and her most comfortable black bra.

A low whistle sounded behind her. Ashlinn whirled around, emitting a sound that was a mixture of a gasp and a squeak, although the situation definitely merited a full-bodied scream.

For sitting in the chair in the corner of the room was Flint, his dark eyes studying her intently.

"What are you doing here?" she demanded breathlessly. "How did you get in?"

She felt vulnerable and exposed, though most models showed far more skin in lingerie catalogs. Ashlinn grabbed her bright blue sweater and held it in front of her in an attempt to shield herself from him.

The aura of intimacy engulfed her. She was alone with Flint, clad only in her underwear, and the hungry glint in his eyes as he watched her made her quiver. Ashlinn clutched the sweater tighter as he rose to his feet and walked toward her, trying to ignore the rush of urgency that streaked through her, realizing that there were some things impossible to ignore.

"I have a key." He stopped in front of her and took the sweater from her, tossing it onto the nearby desk. "And I came up the stairs. They're much faster than the elevator."

"You're supposed to be with our guests." Ashlinn gulped as he put his hands on her hips. His fingertips slipped beneath the waistband of her panties.

"When I left, our guests were deep in discussion about whether or not the cake should be cut without the bride and groom present."

He idly stroked her skin, drawing invisible intricate patterns with the pads of his fingers.

Each movement he made sent a throbbing excitement twisting through her body. It pooled between her legs in aching anticipation. Ashlinn caught her breath and clenched her fists.

"No!" she whispered, even as she wondered why she was whispering. And why she was saying no to her husband.

"They shouldn't cut the cake without the bride and groom present?" Flint deliberately misunderstood her. "Then I guess we'd better get back down there so that everybody will get some dessert."

All the while he was speaking, his hands moved lower until they closed over the rounded curves of her bottom. He began a sensuous, kneading rhythm while she stood there, in passionate thrall.

She bit down on her lower lip, fighting the increasing urge to arch against him, to raise her arms from her sides and wrap them around him. To spread her legs and wriggle against his fingers, inviting, encouraging him to seek greater intimacies.

The force of her desire, of her own wild need scared her, evoking the opposite response to the one she wanted to give.

"No, Flint. Stop it." She jerked her head up and forced her heavy lids to open wide. "I already said there's to be no sex. We…"

"…haven't had any for the past five days," Flint cut in. "If you'll give me a minute to do a quick calculation, I can give you the exact number of hours, too."

"I meant no sex until—until after the baby is born," she said shakily. "Then, if we decide that we still want to be married, we might think about a—a sexual relationship."

Flint's lips twitched. "Think about it, huh?"

She watched him closely, saw his expressions change as she issued her decree. She interpreted surprise, disbelief and incredulity and braced herself for a bout of frustrated-male fury.

It didn't come. "That's nuts, Ashlinn," he said matter-of-factly. "We're married, and we're staying married, so there's nothing to think about."

He pulled her into the masculine cradle of his body, letting her feel the hard power of his erection. "I was willing to give you space while we prepared for the wedding and the move. I figured you needed it. But now, you need something else even more. And so do I. This."

His mouth covered hers and he kissed her, tasting and teasing her lips, her tongue, nibbling and sucking and rubbing until she was clinging to him, writhing against him in urgent abandon.

He slipped a finger inside her, finding the right spot instantly, making her gasp. The familiar pulsing tension that he so ef-

fortlessly evoked in her kept growing, building. She was help-
less against it, against him, and she forgot why she'd thought
this wasn't a good thing.

Because it felt wonderful, she felt wonderful... She couldn't
get enough of what he was doing, and she wanted more.

"Please, Flint," she whimpered.

He felt so good against her, his body strong and powerful,
but she knew how much better it could be. She wanted to feel
his skin bare against hers, she wanted him deep, deep inside
her.

Frantically, she tugged at his shirt, at his belt, trying to free
him from his clothes.

"Oh, Flint, I—I can't wait," she heard herself say, knowing
that she would be embarrassed to remember that she'd been so
utterly uninhibited. Yet she didn't care.

"You don't have to, sweet." His voice was deep, his mouth
close to her ear. "Don't wait."

And she didn't, she couldn't. The exquisite tension abruptly
shattered in an erotic explosion, sending hot glowing ripples
of pleasure through her body. She went limp, her legs too rub-
bery to support her. Fortunately, Flint was there to hold her
and he didn't let her go.

He sat down on the bed with her on his lap, and Ashlinn lay
languorously against him. He stroked her long dark hair until
her breathing resumed a steady pace. When she opened her
eyes, she saw Flint gazing down at her.

He dropped a kiss on the top of her head. "You'd better get
dressed so we can eat a quick piece of cake and make our
goodbyes to the family. Like Rafe said, we have the travel day
from hell ahead of us."

Ashlinn sat up straight. On his lap, she could feel his body,
still taut with arousal, while she was replete and sated to near
torpor. She thought how fast she'd lost control while he remained firmly in possession of his.

"I didn't know we were leaving today. You should have
told me earlier, Flint."

"How long did you think we were going to stick around

here, Ashlinn? All your things have been shipped, we're married.... Why would we stay in New York any longer?''

He sounded so reasonable, so patient. Ashlinn envied his composure. Why couldn't she make him lose his cool? ''Well, I told you I'm not leaving today,'' she announced. ''And I'm not.''

''You also told me you wouldn't have sex,'' he pointed out. ''And although what we just did might not be considered sex in certain circles, it qualifies in mine.''

Ashlinn blushed scarlet. ''I was certainly easy, wasn't I?'' she muttered crossly. ''And you're a big creep to rub it in.''

''I wasn't. I was just making a point.'' He stood up, still holding her in his arms. ''Do you need help getting dressed, Mrs. Paradise?''

''Don't call me that!''

''Ms. Paradise, then?'' He handed her her sweater and she tugged it on. What choice did she have? She couldn't stand around in her underwear!

''No. And if you don't stop with the condescension, I'll...'' she paused, trying to think of a consequence dire enough to satisfy her. And unsettle him!

''...take me for a carriage ride in Central Park?'' Flint feigned real fear.

He made her laugh out loud, damn him.

Ashlinn snatched her leggings and stomped into the bathroom to put them on. But the image of Flint, looking ill-at-ease and touristy trotting through the park in a horse-drawn carriage stayed with her. And maintaining a rotten mood was impossible when she kept wanting to snicker.

Finally, she settled for silently accompanying Flint to his room while he changed into his traveling clothes; khaki slacks and a chambray shirt he'd purchased to wear during his extended stay in New York. He didn't seem inclined to make small talk, so she wasn't sure if he realized that she was snubbing him.

They returned to the private party room where the cake had yet to be cut.

"We just couldn't cut your wedding cake without you,"
Courtney explained. "Although Sarah was all for it."

To Ashlinn, the next hour passed quickly in a blur of kaleidoscope images. She and Flint cut the cake while the photographer clicked away, taking the traditional pictures of them
holding the knife together and feeding each other cake. Then
there were the goodbyes to everybody but Rafe, who rode in
the taxi with her and Flint to the airport.

They traveled coach, with Ashlinn in the crowded middle
seat between the brothers.

"Why didn't you make reservations in first class for at least
some of this trip?" complained Rafe as he attempted to adjust
his long legs to the limited space.

"Paradise Outdoors didn't grow from a small niche company
to one with international sales by reckless spending on frivo-
lous things like first-class airline seats," grumbled Ashlinn,
feeling a moment's solidarity with Rafe. She was trying to
commandeer some armrest space.

"That's exactly right, Ashlinn," Flint said proudly, as if she
were the star pupil in a class of one. "See why she's so perfect
for me, Rafe?"

"She was being sarcastic, Flint," Rafe felt obliged to point
out.

"Not my sweet beautiful bride," exclaimed Flint, placing
his hand on her thigh and freeing the armrest between him and
Ashlinn.

She quickly claimed it.

Rafe turned his attention to a law journal and Ashlinn leafed
through a copy of *Newsweek*. Flint watched Ashlinn, his dark
eyes tracking her every movement.

When she put the magazine away and leaned her head back,
her eyes closing, he flipped up the armrest and drew her to
him. Her head seemed to rest naturally in the hollow of his
shoulder and she surrendered to the wave of exhaustion that
crashed over her.

"Mrs. Paradise," Flint murmured, staring down at her in
something akin to wonder.

Rafe overheard him. "I'm happy for you, Flint. I think she's good for you. And vice versa, I'm sure."

"She's pregnant, Rafe."

"Yeah." Rafe cleared his throat. "Holly guessed. We're both real excited about it," he added warmly.

"I—hope Holly will be friends with Ashlinn." Flint looked troubled. "It wasn't easy for her to leave New York and her job and friends and all. I hope she won't hate living in Sioux Falls—with, uh, me."

It helped to admit his worry to his brother. He could never tell Ashlinn, he had to project enough confidence for the both of them. She was skittish enough about the entire situation, and if he were to express any doubts...

Flint swallowed. "I want it to work out with her, Rafe."

"It will," Rafe assured him. "You've never failed at anything in your life, Flint. I mean, look at what you've done with Paradise Outdoors."

"That's business, Rafe, that's different. I'm no good at relationships." He laughed without mirth. "The only ones who tolerate me are you and Eva."

"You know that isn't true."

"Sure it is. And I never minded before. But now," he took Ashlinn's hand in his own, folding his fingers over hers. "Now I do."

Ten

For the first time since she was fifteen years old Ashlinn was unemployed. She'd worked since landing her first real job, after school and weekends at a frozen yogurt franchise. Even before that, she'd had regular baby-sitting gigs.

"I've never *not* worked," she told Flint on her first day in Sioux Falls. Panic assailed her. "I worked in a clothes store all through college and right after I graduated I went to work for *Tour & Travel*. What am I supposed to do for money? How am I going to pay back my student loans? I hate being in debt but at least I was working my way out of it. Now…"

"How much do you owe on them?" Flint paused in the tying of his tie.

He was getting a late start to the office on his first morning back from his New York stay. Last night, he and Ashlinn had arrived at his apartment too late and tired from their endless trip to do anything but collapse into his king-sized bed. This morning, however…

His lips curved into a satisfied smile. This morning he had

awakened hot and hard with Ashlinn sleeping temptingly close to him in the middle of the bed. Unable not to, he had slowly awakened and aroused her. She had come to him, passionate and loving, as they consummated their marriage.

For the first time ever, that corny retro poster proclaiming something about this being "the first day of the rest of your life" actually made sense to him.

For the first time ever, he wasn't eager to get to the office. His apartment, a place where he never lingered, held a whole new appeal with Ashlinn in it.

His eyes met hers in the bathroom mirror as she told him the amount of her student loans. He shrugged at the five-figure number. "Don't worry about it. Consider it paid."

"What?"

"I'll pay off your loans. You don't think I'd let my wife default on good old Uncle Sam, do you?"

Ashlinn considered not accepting his amazingly generous offer—for about thirty seconds. "Thank you," she said solemnly. "You don't have to, you know." She fiddled with the navy silk belt of her robe. "I'd be stupid not to accept. Not to mention crazy."

"Mmm. Not to mention that. Get the necessary paperwork for me and I'll take care of everything."

"You always seem to be taking care of me," she blurted. It would be so easy to become completely dependent on him. Because of this move, financially she already was. *Hooked!* flashed to mind. When did dependency become addiction?

"I want to get a job, Flint."

"Okay." He ran a brush through his thick black hair.

Ashlinn was taken aback. Though she wasn't sure why, she'd expected an argument. "You don't care?"

"I'm not stepping into that trap." Flint wryly arched his brows. "Of course, I care what you do. But I don't mind if you have a job."

He leaned down to kiss her. She surprised him by leaning into him and holding him tight. Her fervid response to his kiss ended up delaying his return to the office by another hour.

* * *

At first she perused the classifieds in the newspaper daily. There didn't seem to be any job available that she was interested in or one that she wasn't over- or under-qualified for.

"I suppose I could always go back to selling frozen yogurt or clothes at the mall, or even baby-sitting," Ashlinn said gloomily over their Chinese take-out dinner one night.

She was getting tired of takeout, though there was a variety to choose from, and Flint never complained.

Today, she'd almost taken the car and driven to the supermarket because she felt the urge to cook something for dinner. She had restrained herself, however. After years of not owning a car in New York, she was still a little nervous about driving, even in a small city that Flint assured her was "driver-friendly."

The idea of cooking for Flint was pretty unnerving too. It seemed like a scene right out of one of those black-and-white fifties sitcoms shown on *Nick at Nite*. What would come next, Flint arriving at the end of the day calling, "Honey, I'm home"?

"I have to have a job, Flint," she repeated her mantra.

"Well, there's always Paradise Outdoors."

"Work for you?" Ashlinn stared at him, astounded. "Doing what?"

"I don't know. We could find something. Carmody is always coming up with ideas and he's forever trying to expand his power base. I'm sure he'd be delighted to have you in marketing."

It made sense, but all at once, Ashlinn wasn't in a hurry to start. Just knowing there was a job waiting for her provided a security that enabled her to do other things first.

She set up an appointment with an obstetrician recommended by Holly, which made the baby seem more real. And made Flint's one-bedroom, sparsely furnished apartment begin to feel ridiculously inadequate.

"We have to get a bigger place," Ashlinn told him one night as they lay in each other's arms after long, satisfying lovemaking. "I'd like to get my things out of storage, and with the baby coming…"

"Of course." Flint splayed his fingers possessively over the tiny swell of her belly. "The baby. When do you get that sonogram that tells if it's a boy or girl?"

They'd had dinner last night with Rafe and Holly, who had brought him up to speed on such things. Ashlinn already knew quite a bit from Michelle and Courtney's pregnancies.

"At around five months. Courtney and Connor didn't want to know and asked the doctor not to tell them the baby's sex. Michelle and Steve did know with the twins."

"I'd like to know what it is as soon as possible," Flint said decisively, then seemed to remember that his wasn't the only vote. "Do you?"

"Definitely. I guess you want a boy?"

"There's a sexist assumption. I guess that means you want a girl, Ashlinn?"

"I just want a healthy child," she retorted.

"So do I. If it's a girl, I hope she's just like you," he said thoughtfully. "And if it's a boy, I hope he's like Rafe."

Ashlinn raised her head from his chest and impulsively kissed his cheek. "I hope he's just like his daddy."

They began house-hunting because Flint said it made more sense to buy their own place than to rent a larger apartment. Ashlinn did most of the looking in the company of a vivacious real estate agent with a remarkable ability to enthuse over everything that was shown. Flint went only to those places Ashlinn thought he might like, which happened to be the ones she liked most herself.

Eventually they found a brick-and-siding house in an expanding development outside the city, with easy access to the interstate highway. It had everything Ashlinn had never even realized she wanted in a house, but there was one key flaw.

Rafe and Holly's house was less than three blocks away which meant that Kaylin was too, along with Camryn when she came home on vacation.

Ashlinn didn't really mind. She liked Rafe and Holly a lot.
They seemed like older, wiser siblings to her, and despite
Flint's heated assertions to the contrary, his teenaged half sis-
ters weren't all that bad. Camryn had made a special trip back
from Vermillion to get acquainted with Ashlinn, and she'd seen
Kaylin several times while visiting Holly and Rafe.

The girls were friendly, ready to forget all about that first
memorable meeting and welcome Ashlinn into the Paradise
family. It didn't take Ashlinn very long to figure out that Camryn and Kaylin accepted her so wholeheartedly because Eva,
their perpetual foe, was alleged to be furious about Flint's startling, sudden marriage.

Eva, doing a medical school rotation in Rapid City, was
scheduled to return to Sioux Falls when the semester ended
just before Christmas. Until then, she had no plans to come
back, even for a day, and especially not to meet her new sister-
in-law. She did ask Flint to come to visit her because she
missed him terribly.

Her being rejected by Eva cemented the younger girls' loyalty to Ashlinn.

"Wait till you meet Eva. You'll hate her," Kaylin exclaimed
eagerly. "Maybe as much as she hates you!"

"How can Eva hate me when she's never even met me?"
Ashlinn intended the question to be rhetorical, but Kaylin proceeded to answer it.

"Because you exist, Ashlinn, and worse, you married her
big brother. If you really want to make her crazy, insist on
going to Rapid City with Flint when he goes to see her." Kaylin's dark Paradise eyes glowed. "That'll totally ruin her visit
with him!"

Ashlinn remembered Eva's *"sophisticated women take sexual responsibility"* dig and for a moment, she was tempted.
But her better nature prevailed. "I don't want to ruin anything
for anybody, Kaylin. Anyway, Flint has no plans to go to Rapid
City, as far as I know."

The next day, Flint told Ashlinn he planned to visit Eva in
Rapid City next weekend and invited her to go along. "I know

Eva is anxious to meet you, but her work and study schedule makes it impossible for her to come back here,'' he explained.

Ashlinn wondered if Flint was hopelessly dense regarding his younger sister or if the teenaged girls used Eva as a convenient scapegoat in their own difficult relationship with Flint.

She tried to tactfully ask Holly about their mutual sister-in-law but Holly replied with equal tact, ''Flint has a bit of a blind spot where Eva is concerned. And Eva has certain…abandonment issues to work through.''

Not much information, but it was the deciding factor in Ashlinn's decision not to go to Rapid City with Flint. ''You should go and spend some time alone with your sister,'' she said, feeling generous. ''Especially since you won't be here at Christmas. Mom and Dad are so happy we're going to Florida to spend the holidays with them.''

She had been worried that Flint wouldn't want to leave Sioux Falls and Paradise Outdoors over Christmas, but he had immediately agreed to the trip south.

''Catalog sales are biggest before the holidays, not during, and I want to be with you when you tell your folks about the baby. Do you think they'll count backwards from our wedding day?''

''If they do, they'll never admit it. Michelle's twins were born less than nine months after their wedding and they weren't preemies. Nobody's ever said a word.''

Her answer satisfied him.

As for the house, he liked it enough to buy it.

Transforming a house into a home took a lot of time and effort, especially when there were also preparations for a new baby that needed to be made. Ashlinn was surprised to realize she was enjoying her new-found domesticity.

She shopped for the house, for herself and the baby and Flint. She took more of an interest in cooking and scoffed at her earlier refusal to prepare meals. *What had she been afraid of?* she mused, but didn't look too deeply for answers.

Married sex kept getting better and better, not that it hadn't been good to begin with. But the sexual bond between them grew beyond physical intimacy into an emotional closeness that was more deeply satisfying than anything Ashlinn had ever experienced. She'd rarely let herself depend on others, neither had Flint.

But she began to rely on him coming home to her every day and on the security of their routine: spending evenings together eating and talking, laughing and making love. Weekends were much the same, with additional activities like working on the house, going to the movies, even occasionally socializing with other couples in the neighborhood.

Ashlinn was happy and content; sometimes she was stunned by just how much. Other times she worried about it. She wondered if Flint felt the same way.

It was something they didn't talk about. Their conversations were easy and open but didn't include analyzing feelings. The pragmatic and introverted Flint would never initiate what he considered a pointless discussion. As the author of *Hooked!*, which fell into a category Holly dubbed "sham psychology," Ashlinn was reluctant to make another venture into that particular territory herself.

So she didn't tell her husband she loved him and that she loved being his wife, and she tried not to mind that he never mentioned loving her, either. There was a lot for her to be thankful for and plenty to keep her busy, and Ashlinn tried to keep focused on that.

She had never expected to find such satisfaction in being a wife and mother-to-be and she considered putting her plans to work on hold. "Maybe I should just concentrate on being a mother for a while," she tentatively suggested to Flint.

"Sure," said Flint. "Whatever you want, Ashlinn. As long as you're happy."

"I am." And then Flint kissed her, completely derailing her train of thought and bringing their discussion to a passionate close.

Flint didn't associate Christmas with palm trees and sun and summer clothes, but he savored the holiday in South Florida with Ashlinn and her parents. Adding to his pleasure was the stunningly successful season Paradise Outdoors had enjoyed, with catalog orders up, and from all over the world.

Only Koji's article had been published so far, and it was expected that sales would increase even more after additional exposure in the articles by Hall and Bouvier and Rico, all due out in the coming months. The four adventurers sent their congratulations to Flint and Ashlinn upon hearing of their marriage. All four claimed they weren't surprised.

Flint and Ashlinn spent an idyllic week in Florida together. They walked along the beach holding hands, they swam in the ocean and in the pool near the Careys' home, they visited an orange grove and drank lots of fresh juice. At night they made love, trying to stay discreetly quiet in deference to her parents just down the hall. It was a challenge that invariably ended in muffled laughter along with muffled moans and sighs.

The Careys were delighted with the news about the baby and didn't mention any correlation between their wedding date and her due date.

Flint never thought about it himself anymore. He was deeply in love with his wife and couldn't imagine not having her in his life. Though he held no New Age beliefs, it all seemed pre-ordained in some kind of karmic way—the camping expedition, the night in the lake, the instant pregnancy.

It was as if his emotional life had been on ice while he waited for them to meet. He'd never felt this way about anyone, hadn't thought himself capable of such intensity, except in regards to his company, of course. But Ashlinn engaged him on every level. He didn't just crave the sensual pleasures of her body, that would never be enough for him now. Now he wanted the whole woman, everything about her, her warmth and her wit and her honesty. Even her sarcasm and crankiness was preferable to anyone else's best.

Most of all he wanted her love.

Sometimes he was sure she loved him; other times he wasn't quite so confident. As Eva had pointed out during his visit to her in Rapid City, it was easy to confuse gratitude with love. And Ashlinn was grateful to him, Eva declared frankly. Why wouldn't she be? He gave her everything she wanted.

Flint didn't dispute it nor was he ashamed to admit it. Whatever he gave to Ashlinn, he gave freely. He didn't want her to worry about her student loans so he'd paid them off for her. He wanted her to have the house that she wanted, to buy whatever she felt was needed for it. He wanted her to have a car so she would have the freedom to go when and where she pleased, so he'd bought her a car.

He simply considered himself a good husband, like Rafe was to Holly, but Eva teased that he was more like a fairy godmother than a husband.

"Your marriage is very different from Rafe's," Eva explained. "Holly works like a plowhorse, bringing in extra income from her practice, taking care of those foster children, plus our bratty half sisters. Rafe needs her around, so naturally he tries to placate her. It's the opposite for you, Flint. It seems to me that Ashlinn is the one who takes while you give and give and give."

"It's not like that at all," Flint protested testily, but he couldn't find the words to tell his little sister everything that Ashlinn brought to his life. It was too personal, too private, strictly between him and his wife.

Anyway, his anger dissolved when Eva threw her arms around him. "I just don't want you to get hurt, Flint. You're my big brother and I love you so much."

"I love you too, Eva," he'd said. Strange, how it was easy to say the words to his kid sister, yet impossible to say to his wife.

He longed to say, "I love you, Ashlinn," but deliberately held back. If she was merely grateful to him, she wouldn't want to be burdened with a declaration of love. Being Ashlinn, she might even interpret it as manipulation, and that would infuriate her.

The last thing he wanted was to transform a love scene into a raging fight. He and Ashlinn didn't argue much anymore.

In the months since their wedding, they had grown remarkably compatible and congenial.

No, he wasn't going to mess things up by telling her he loved her.

Back home in Sioux Falls after the holidays in gray cold January, Flint suggested inviting Eva to their house for dinner. She was in the Sioux Falls area for her final semester before graduating from medical school in June, and the sisters-in-law had yet to meet.

With some trepidation, Ashlinn phoned Eva to extend the invitation. Eva was cool but accepted the invitation. Ashlinn called her mother for some "idiot-proof recipes that nobody, not even me, can mess up."

As usual, her mom came through. Whatever else happened during this crucial meeting with Eva, at least the food would be edible.

Eva arrived a few minutes late for their dinner. It was definitely a relief to see that her new sister-in-law didn't possess any visible demonic qualities, Ashlinn mused whimsically. In looks, Eva was a combination of Flint and Rafe—and of Camryn and Kaylin, too. Ashlinn decided it would be wise not to point this out to any of them, however.

She noticed Eva giving her an equally thorough once-over. "Not to worry. Satan won't be summoning me back to hell at any given moment," Ashlinn said dryly.

Eva blushed. "I can't even imagine what you must think of me, considering what you've heard from *them*."

That was a topic Ashlinn had no intention of touching; she wasn't about to get dragged into the Paradise sisters' seemingly never-ending feud. She quickly passed the plate of her mom's fail-safe Hot 'n Cheesy hors d'oeuvres while asking the doctor-to-be some pertinent questions about dairy products. Eva enthusiastically launched into a detailed discussion about the values of cheese.

Dinner passed uneventfully. Afterward, Eva even offered to

help with the dishes, dispatching her brother to his computer in the den. He went without comment.

"I don't want you to think that I'm one of those women who believe that men should be excused from kitchen duties," Eva stated as she and Ashlinn began the cleanup. "Ordinarily, I'd insist that Flint be right in here helping us."

"Ordinarily, he is," Ashlinn said wryly. "I'm not one of those women who believe men should be excused from kitchen duties, either."

"Oh." Eva paused, then took a deep breath. "The truth is, I just wanted a little time alone with you, Ashlinn." The words seemed to pour out of her. "I can guess the kinds of things Camryn and Kaylin have been telling you, things I might've said that they—uh—might've misinterpreted." She gulped.

Ashlinn took pity on her. "Eva, I know you love Flint very much and I know the girls are prone to—misinterpretations. I'm just glad that we finally met."

"Oh, so am I! I've been so worried about Flint. Certain things he said led me to believe... You see, he was acting totally out of character and then you were married so suddenly. I didn't know what was going on and so I thought—I was afraid that—" Eva heaved a sigh. "I made some very wrong assumptions, Ashlinn. I apologize."

Ashlinn smiled. "As one who's made some really wrong assumptions myself, I'm more than happy to forgive and forget all about it, Eva."

"I can't tell you what a relief it is to know that I was wrong about you. I can see that you love my brother and he loves you and—"

"You can see that Flint loves me?" Ashlinn's voice trembled. If only it were true! But she was hesitant to believe. After all, Eva's talent for making wrong assumptions rivaled her own.

Eva picked up on her uncertainty at once. "You don't think Flint loves you?" Her relieved expression was fast replaced with one of concern. "Why not?"

"I'm having a baby," Ashlinn said bluntly. "Flint might've

already told you or maybe you guessed, but that's the only reason he married me. And it might be—it probably is—just a temporary situation for him.''

''Temporary?'' Eva echoed. ''But he bought a house!''

''He has to live somewhere and a house is a good investment. It really doesn't have anything to do with me.''

''So you see him as trapped in an inconvenient marriage of convenience?'' Eva frowned. ''I have to tell you, Ashlinn, that doesn't sound like my brother. Flint isn't one to do things he really doesn't want to do. He and I are a lot alike that way.''

''How right you are, Eva.'' Flint joined them, his face dark as a blizzard sky. His tone was as chilling as the winter wind blowing outside.

''Were you eavesdropping on our private conversation, Flint?'' demanded Eva.

''You were gossiping about what is a very private matter.'' Flint ignored his sister and glowered at Ashlinn. ''Do you dissect me like that with Holly and the girls, too?''

''Of course not!'' Ashlinn was defensive. ''We were just— just—'' She lapsed into silence. She really had been dissecting him with Eva. Her cheeks burned.

''I have so much studying to do,'' interjected Eva. ''If I don't leave right now, I'll be up all night. Thanks for the dinner and—'bye!'' She made a speedy exit, leaving the newlyweds alone together.

Ashlinn went upstairs to escape Flint's hard-eyed stare. He was angry with her, she knew, but his anger seemed way out of proportion to the meager crime of discussing him with his sister. Maybe what they'd said had struck a nerve, had hurt his pride. Maybe he hadn't wanted his beloved little sister to know the truth about them...

She changed into her nightgown and was wondering whether to go back downstairs to Flint or just give up and go to bed when he appeared at the doorway.

Ashlinn faced him, her pulses hammering. ''Are you still mad?'' she asked lightly, striving to defuse the tension.

''Shouldn't I be?'' He crossed the room and stood in front

of her. "Do you honestly believe that I bought this place because I considered owning a house to be a good investment?
That this—all of this—has nothing to do with you?"

Ashlinn felt her baby move inside her, as if to urge her on.
She had to ask, she couldn't go any longer without knowing
for sure. She lifted her head and met Flint's eyes. "Flint, I—
I have a question, too. Do you love me?"

"How can you even ask that?" Flint demanded thickly.
"Don't you know? I've done everything I could to show you
how I feel about you. Of course, I love you, Ashlinn. I love
you so much that it doesn't matter if you don't love me back.
Just stay with me and maybe someday…"

Tears filled her eyes and Ashlinn didn't try to fight them,
she let them roll down her cheeks. "Oh Flint, I do love you.
I wanted to tell you but I…" she gave her head an impatient
shake. "I can't exactly remember why I thought I shouldn't
tell you. I fell in love with you while we were camping and
ever since, I've been wanting you to love me, too."

"Sweetheart, I do." He scooped her up in his arms and laid
her down on the bed.

They kissed as they quickly undressed, too starved for each
other to stay apart. Ashlinn pulled him down on the bed, ready
for him, aching for him. She cried his name as he thrust inside
her with a primal, sexy sound of arousal.

They moved together, sweet hot friction, madly pleasurable
in its fullness. He was deep, deep inside her and she thrilled
to his possession. Holding back was not an option for either of
them. They were swept away on a sensual tidal wave that carried them high and finally sent them drifting in the sweet seas
of rapture.

Finally, they collapsed together, breathless.

Flint wrapped his arms around her, spooning her. "There is
nothing temporary about our marriage, Ashlinn," he murmured
against her ear. He lifted a handful of her hair and pressed a
tender kiss on her neck. "And it's not a marriage based on
convenience or inconvenience or whatever. It's permanent and
it's based on love. Got that?"

"Got it." She squeezed his hand that rested on her belly. "But that doesn't mean we won't ever fight again," she felt obliged to explain. "Even though we love each other, you know we will."

"What we won't do is let anything come between us," Flint pledged.

"No, never," Ashlinn agreed drowsily. She drifted off to sleep, secure in her husband's love.

Madison Carey Paradise was born on the fifth of April, a dark-haired, dark-eyed six-pound-eight-ounce beauty.

A day later her three Paradise aunts lined up at the nursery window to admire her.

"She looks just like me as a baby," said Camryn.

"No, she doesn't. She looks exactly like me as a baby," argued Kaylin.

"You two looked like drowned rats when you were born." Eva was scornful. "It's obvious from baby pictures that little Madison is a virtual clone of me as an infant."

Flint and Ashlinn, walking down the corridor hand in hand, overheard the discussion.

"Maddie looks like her mother," Flint pronounced, drawing Ashlinn close. "Absolutely beautiful."

Nobody disagreed. As Flint and Ashlinn gazed raptly at their daughter through the glass, the three Paradise sisters looked on with angelic smiles.

*   *   *   *   *

Don't miss Silhouette's newest cross-line promotion,

Four royal sisters find their own Prince Charmings as they embark on separate journeys to find their missing brother, the Crown Prince!

The search begins in October 1999 and continues through February 2000:

On sale October 1999: **A ROYAL BABY ON THE WAY** by award-winning author **Susan Mallery** (Special Edition)

On sale November 1999: **UNDERCOVER PRINCESS** by bestselling author **Suzanne Brockmann** (Intimate Moments)

On sale December 1999: **THE PRINCESS'S WHITE KNIGHT** by popular author **Carla Cassidy** (Romance)

On sale January 2000: **THE PREGNANT PRINCESS** by rising star **Anne Marie Winston** (Desire)

On sale February 2000: **MAN...MERCENARY...MONARCH** by top-notch talent **Joan Elliott Pickart** (Special Edition)

ROYALLY WED
Only in—
SILHOUETTE BOOKS

Available at your favorite retail outlet.

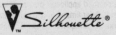

Visit us at www.romance.net

SSERW

If you enjoyed what you just read,
then we've got an offer you can't resist!

Take 2 bestselling love stories FREE!

Plus get a FREE surprise gift!

Clip this page and mail it to Silhouette Reader Service™

IN U.S.A.	IN CANADA
3010 Walden Ave.	P.O. Box 609
P.O. Box 1867	Fort Erie, Ontario
Buffalo, N.Y. 14240-1867	L2A 5X3

YES! Please send me 2 free Silhouette Desire® novels and my free surprise gift. Then send me 6 brand-new novels every month, which I will receive months before they're available in stores. In the U.S.A., bill me at the bargain price of $3.12 plus 25¢ delivery per book and applicable sales tax, if any*. In Canada, bill me at the bargain price of $3.49 plus 25¢ delivery per book and applicable taxes**. That's the complete price and a savings of over 10% off the cover prices—what a great deal! I understand that accepting the 2 free books and gift places me under no obligation ever to buy any books. I can always return a shipment and cancel at any time. Even if I never buy another book from Silhouette, the 2 free books and gift are mine to keep forever. So why not take us up on our invitation. You'll be glad you did!

225 SEN CNFA

326 SEN CNFC

Name	(PLEASE PRINT)	
Address	Apt.#	
City	State/Prov.	Zip/Postal Code

* Terms and prices subject to change without notice. Sales tax applicable in N.Y.

** Canadian residents will be charged applicable provincial taxes and GST.
   All orders subject to approval. Offer limited to one per household.
   ® are registered trademarks of Harlequin Enterprises Limited.

DES99   ©1998 Harlequin Enterprises Limited

THE FORTUNES OF TEXAS

*Membership in this family has
its privileges…and its price.
But what a fortune can't buy,
a true-bred Texas love is sure to bring!*

Coming in November 1999…

Expecting…
In Texas

by

MARIE FERRARELLA

Wrangler Cruz Perez's night of passion with Savannah Clark
had left the beauty pregnant with his child. Cruz's cowboy
code of honor demanded he do right by the expectant
mother, but could he convince Savannah—and himself—
that his offer of marriage was inspired by true love?

THE FORTUNES OF TEXAS continues with
A Willing Wife by Jackie Merritt,
available in December 1999 from
Silhouette Books.

Available at your favorite retail outlet.

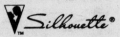

Visit us at www.romance.net

PSFOT3

In November 1999 share in the holiday magic as the national bestseller that captured readers' hearts is now in paperback for the first time—with an added bonus!

LONE STAR
Christmas...
AND OTHER GIFTS

Bestselling authors
DIANA PALMER
and
JOAN JOHNSTON

come together in one special Christmas collection that brings readers four wonderful stories brimming with dazzling romance and fiery passion.

Celebrate Christmas with four devastatingly handsome heroes, including a most memorable *Long, Tall Texan* and an infamous outlaw from *Hawk's Way*.

A Christmas keepsake to treasure always!

Available at your favorite retail outlet.

Silhouette®

Visit us at www.romance.net

PSLSC

SILHOUETTE® *Desire*®

COMING NEXT MONTH